"Do y

Terry claimed her waist with his arm.

As if she stood outside herself, Karen watched them dancing, two dark figures silhouetted against a sparkly silver world. At the same time, she felt his body moving, his thigh brushing hers, his hand pressing her waist. His cheek grazed her hair as they glided through the waltz like an ethereal Fred Astaire and Ginger Rogers.

His nearness shaped a series of electric tingles along her shoulders and breasts. Their limbs entwined and yet they never stumbled.

She had the sensation that he was making love to her without removing their clothes.

ABOUT THE AUTHOR

Jacqueline Diamond lives in Brea, California. Her house is stuffed with one hundred and one pasta recipes and populated by her husband and two young sons. She spends her spare time chasing raccoons out of the tomatoes, scaring birds off the apple tree and dreaming up weird ideas to write about.

Books by Jacqueline Diamond
HARLEQUIN AMERICAN ROMANCE

218—UNLIKELY PARTNERS
239—THE CINDERELLA DARE
270—CAPERS AND RAINBOWS
279—A GHOST OF A CHANCE
315—FLIGHT OF MAGIC
351—BY LEAPS AND BOUNDS
406—OLD DREAMS, NEW DREAMS

Don't miss any of our special offers. Write to us at the following address for information on our newest releases.

Harlequin Reader Service
P.O. Box 1397, Buffalo, NY 14240
Canadian address: P.O. Box 603,
Fort Erie, Ont. L2A 5X3

JACQUELINE DIAMOND

THE TROUBLE WITH TERRY

Harlequin Books

TORONTO • NEW YORK • LONDON
AMSTERDAM • PARIS • SYDNEY • HAMBURG
STOCKHOLM • ATHENS • TOKYO • MILAN
MADRID • WARSAW • BUDAPEST • AUCKLAND

For Jane Browne, superagent

Published July 1992

ISBN 0-373-16446-7

THE TROUBLE WITH TERRY

Chapter One

A child's heartbroken wail filled the parking lot.

Karen pulled her car into its slot in front of Michaels' Real Estate. She'd overstayed her lunch break running errands, but she had to make sure the child was all right.

A check revealed a little girl about three years old standing in front of the supermarket, wearing a denim jumpsuit and clutching a bottle of soap bubbles. As Karen swung out of the car, she saw a man bend down beside the youngster.

Around them, shoppers carried out their groceries, while cars cruised by searching for parking places. A clerk, clad in a California Angels T-shirt, perched atop a ladder festooning the lampposts with Christmas bells.

Karen hurried toward the child, dodging a pair of bicycles on the walkway. "Can I help?"

The man looked up. The first thing she noticed were the amazingly bright blue eyes and then the off-center grin. Vaguely she observed a shock of black hair and a green sweatshirt that read "Please, God, Let Me Prove to You That Winning the Lottery Won't Spoil Me."

When the man straightened, her senses registered the lean length of him, each well-defined muscle taut with energy.

"We have a lost child here." His hand shot out. "Terry Vogel."

"Karen Loesser." Without thinking, she extended hers in response. His flesh felt firm and cool, and his lingering touch gave the act of shaking hands an unexpected intimacy.

"This is Belinda." He indicated the child. "She says she hopped out of the van while her mother was loading groceries. Chances are she'll be be missed momentarily."

"I want my Mommy!" Belinda squeezed her bottle of soap bubbles. "I want to go home!"

Karen knelt down. "I'm sure she'll be back soon."

"I don't see any point in calling the police, at least not yet," Terry explained from a point overhead.

He seemed kind, but she knew nothing about him. Karen stood up. "I can handle it from here."

Those brilliant blue eyes gazed directly into hers. "We could share," he said. "It isn't every day I get a chance to do a good deed."

His square shoulders blocked out the sidewalk behind him, and the angle of his body defined a cozy space for the three of them. As if they were a family, instead of strangers.

It made no sense for them both to wait here and obviously she couldn't leave the child with a strange man. But his firm stance and the thrust of the chin left no doubt that he was staying.

"Where's my Mommy?" Belinda recalled their attention.

"She's on her way, I promise." Terry reached for the soap bubbles. "May I borrow this?"

Belinda released the bottle reluctantly. "Why?"

"I'll show you."

No one else paid them any attention, and yet Karen found her own attention riveted on Terry. Beneath his masculine strength she felt an impish sense of mischief waiting to burst out.

Uh-oh. This tickle inside her soul was a warning sign of danger ahead, she knew from experience. Take one tantalizingly attractive man, add a dash of raffish charm, mix with Karen's much too soft heart, and the results were likely to be explosive.

Terry dropped the lid into his pocket and lifted out the bubble wand. "Let me tell you a story," he said.

"Is there a gingerbread man in it?" Belinda balanced on one foot.

"Oh, lots of them." Terry blew with painstaking slowness the biggest bubble Karen had ever seen. Colors refracted in it, setting tiny rainbows dancing in the sunlight.

The bubble clung to the tip of the wand. "Can you see them?" Terry asked.

"Who?" The little girl squinted at the orb.

"What we have here," Terry said, "is a whole gingerbread kingdom. Hundreds of the tiniest gingerbread people ever made."

"I don't—where?" Belinda frowned.

The bubble broke loose and floated earthward, followed by a cloud of globes bobbing and swaying on the wind currents. "They're right in there. Laughing and riding bicycles and dropping water balloons out the windows."

Karen stood motionless, wondering at her own fascination. Whenever she blew bubbles for her two children, she felt as if magic floated just beyond her reach. Today, the air fizzed and glinted with it, close enough to capture.

"Long ago," Terry said, "all the gingerbread men lay flat and still. They weren't really men but cakes and cookies for good children to eat."

"I'm very good," said Belinda. "And I love cookies."

"And then—" a fresh flotilla filled the space around them "—a fairy godmother arrived in Soapland and saw that the children were lonely. They had no toys and no pets to play with."

Belinda caught a bubble on the palm of her hand. She pressed it to her nose and sneezed when it popped. "That feels funny."

"Exactly what the fairy godmother said." Terry's solemn tone had the ironic effect of making Karen smile at his silliness. "She said, 'I feel funny, seeing all these lonely children, while those gingerbread men are just lying around.'"

"But you could eat them," Belinda pointed out.

"Yes, but wouldn't you rather play with them?" Terry waved the wand and prisms rippled. "I would. I'd rather play than eat, any day."

"I want to eat them," Belinda said stubbornly.

Terry gazed up at Karen as if for help. "Yes, but... Okay." He nipped at a soap bubble and then answered himself in a squeaky voice, "Ouch! Ow! Oh, owee! Don't eat us!"

Belinda giggled. "You're doing that. There aren't really any little men in there."

"Ow, ow, ow," said Terry. The little girl giggled some more. "Oh, that's my arm! Don't eat my arm, Mr. Man!"

He halted as a blue van screeched up and a woman leaped out. "Belinda! My God!" The mother grabbed her little girl, alternately hugging and scolding. "How many times have I told you— Are you all right?"

"Do I have to go now?" the child asked. "I want to eat a gingerbread man!"

Terry reassembled the bottle and returned it to its small owner. "But you can't. Because they're alive now and they're protected by the First Amendment."

"What's that?" said Belinda.

"The right of gingerbread men to dance inside soap bubbles without being eaten," Terry said.

"I'm hungry." Belinda hopped up and down.

"Thank you." The mother addressed Karen and Terry over her shoulder as she tugged her wayward daughter into the van. "You've been so kind."

Karen glimpsed a newborn strapped into the front seat and a toddler who couldn't have been more than two peering out the back. No wonder the mother hadn't noticed when Belinda jumped out!

"An adventure." Terry turned to Karen. "I was hoping to have one today. Children can be so refreshingly infuriating. Would you like an ice-cream float or some frozen yogurt or a bottle of rotgut gin, or something?"

"I have to get back to work." She adjusted her purse against her shoulder. She didn't really want to leave, but boyish charm had always been her downfall and she had no intention of falling again. "Thanks—you were great with Belinda."

"I love doing stuff like that." Terry reached out and tugged her sleeve, smoothing a wrinkle beneath the purse strap. "Do you like model-car exhibits? Ice hockey? I could get tickets to something for Saturday."

"I have to go." Karen smiled and hurried off, fleeing the irrational impulse to make a date with this unlikely prospect. The last thing she needed in her life was a man like Terry Vogel.

"See you," he called.

When she reached the door of the real-estate office Karen looked toward the supermarket, but Terry had gone. She swallowed a twinge of regret and marched herself inside.

THE MIDDLE-AGED MAN with scraggly brown hair leaned across Karen's desk with a wink. "Hey, if the boss's out, why don't you give me the real lowdown?"

"Beg pardon?" Karen said frostily, wishing the phone would ring. After that brief enchanted interlude, the afternoon had turned into a clunking bore.

"Yeah. I mean, I see this stuff on TV, about getting rich on foreclosures, you know," the clod was saying. "I'd like to get into something like that."

"George should be back any minute." Karen glanced around the small storefront office, wishing the man would take a hint and leave her alone. She still had to run off mailing labels on the computer, and it was already four-thirty. With the sensation that ginger ale sparkled through her veins, she'd found it hard to buckle down to work.

"Look here." The thin-faced man pulled a crumpled copy of George's newspaper ad from his pocket. It featured half a dozen photographs of houses with one-paragraph blurbs underneath. "This one here, this Victorian."

"It's close to downtown Whittier," Karen recited. "Four bedrooms, two baths. A cosmetic fixer, needs paint and linoleum and a little handyman work. The price is listed right there."

"Yeah, yeah, I know what the ad says." At least the man didn't have bad breath—he was leaning close enough that she would have noticed, if he had. "But I drove by and that paint is really peeling. You ask me, they're probably going into foreclosure. What's the scoop? Think they'd take fifty thousand less than they're asking?"

"No," she said.

"No?" The visitor lifted an eyebrow. "I mean, how would you know? You're just the secretary."

"It's my house," Karen said, and bit back an urge to tell the jerk she wouldn't sell it to *him* for a full-price offer. Not even if he offered to toss rose petals under her feet as she moved out. Her beloved house, the home where she'd brought her babies and nursed them and watched them grow into children, in the hands of this Grade-A creep? Never.

On the other hand, it *had* been on the market for three months.

"Oh," said the man, finally at a loss for words. "Well, I guess I'll wait a few minutes and see if your boss shows up."

"Do that," Karen snapped, and bent to her computer. At the same time the phone rang.

She was in the middle of straightening out a client about the date of an open house when George swung through the door. Dapper, that was the word for her boss, she reflected as she keyed the computer to begin printing labels.

George Michaels was only thirty-nine, ten years older than Karen, but she couldn't imagine that he'd ever been young. He had a well-preserved look, with permanently tanned skin from too much tennis in the sun. Seeing the young man, he smiled automatically, creases radiating from his eyes and mouth.

"George Michaels. What can I do for you?" The broker extended his hand. "Right this way." He swept the client into his office without a glance at Karen.

Twenty minutes later, she was shutting down her computer when George escorted the man out again, shook his hand and said, "You come see me when you've got a down payment."

"Sure thing." The scraggly-haired visitor wandered out.

"He didn't even have a down payment?" Karen asked.

"He may be back someday. You never know." George pulled out a tissue and blew his nose. Allergies again. Although it was the end of November, Southern California gusted with hot Santa Ana winds that stirred up pollen from a long dry season. "Listen, I'm showing your house at seven tonight."

"I'll get it staged." That meant not only cleaning up the toys but turning on all the lights to make the house look roomy and welcoming. Of course it always seemed that way to her, Karen mused as she picked up her purse.

"You're not leaving?" George turned on the threshold of his office.

"It is five o'clock," Karen said.

"Honey, we've simply got to get that mailing out today." George shook his head. "You should have had my fliers posted on Monday and it's Thursday already."

"But you didn't give me the information until yesterday," Karen pointed out. "George, I have to pick up my kids."

"Your sister-in-law won't mind." He waved as he disappeared into his office. "I know I can count on you, Karen."

She gritted her teeth and sank into her chair. Another hour of work, and she still had to get the house tidied up for a buyer. Darn George, and darn Bobby for leaving her in this mess.

Grimly she dialed Marian's number.

The kids would be disappointed, but she'd take them to a hamburger drive-through for dinner. Thinking about how much they'd enjoy the meal, Karen relaxed and was already peeling and sticking labels by the time her sister-in-law answered the phone.

PERFORMING A semiprofessional balancing act, Karen unlocked the front door without dropping the sack of food, her soft drink, her purse or Rose's homework.

Behind her, the children staggered through the door carrying their own burdens—kids' meal boxes, soft drinks, Rose's favorite doll, Bopper's bag of toys.

Watching them head for the dining room, Karen leaned against the door for a minute and wondered why she didn't have a headache. It must be the result of drinking five cups of coffee today; her nerves had long ago taken wing and flown south for the winter.

"Mom?" Rose called. "Would you like me to put out paper plates?"

"Sure." Thank goodness for helpful seven-year-old daughters, Karen thought as she made her way through the living room, stepping over the crayons and coloring books left from the previous night.

It wasn't an elegant living room by modern standards—no cathedral ceilings, no plush carpeting. But Karen had lovingly restored the hardwood flooring and the molding around the mantelpiece.

She'd loved this house since childhood, had studied it every day as she walked by on the way to school. When the opportunity had arisen for her and Bobby to buy it eight years earlier, she'd jumped at the chance, even though the house needed tons of work.

Looking back, Karen could see that Bobby had been suffocating inch by inch as they acquired a mortgage and then children. After he left two years ago, she'd first blamed herself for not realizing the extent of his feelings. But darn it, he was a grown man; he could speak for himself.

Besides, she wasn't sure anything would have held him. The perpetual child, Bobby had cast her in the role of mother figure and then instituted his own rebellion. Well, twenty-seven was too young to mother a twenty-eight-year-old man, and Karen hadn't been interested in trying.

She slipped into her seat in the dining room. The antique-style furnishings blended in with the decor, except for the large wall painting from Bobby's impressionist period. Imitation Monet didn't do much for Karen, but when she'd tried to take it down, the children had cried until she put it back.

She'd make sure she lost the painting when they moved.

"Mommy." Bopper poked a straw into his orange juice. "Is Daddy coming home for Christmas?"

"Oh, Bop-brain!" Rose scolded as she arranged paper napkins beside the plates.

"Is he?" Bopper demanded with a five-year-old's tenacity.

Karen forced herself to swallow the irritation she felt toward her ex-husband. She had made up her mind long ago never to run him down to the children. "It may not be possible," she said. "Oregon's pretty far from Southern California."

"He might send us something." Rose finished laying out the flatware and sat primly in her chair. "Maybe a painting for my room."

"A car!" Bopper cried. "A radio-controlled car!"

"You're not old enough for a radio-controlled car," Rose said.

"Jason and Fred have them!"

"They're five and a *half,*" Rose sniffed.

"Where shall we get our tree this year?" Karen interjected. "Maybe they'll be selling them at the high school again."

"I want a white one," Bopper said through a mouthful of hamburger.

"They're so tacky." Rose ate her french fries with a fork, as if they were sticks of asparagus. "Mommy, can I get a bridal gown for my Barbie doll?"

"It's on the list," Karen promised. "Listen, kids, George is bringing a buyer tonight. They should be here in half an hour."

"No, they won't," Rose said. "George is always late."

"I hope they don't show up at all!" Bopper blew through his straw, churning up his juice. "What's

Daddy going to think when he comes home and we're not here?''

"He'll have our new address," Karen assured him, squeezing more ranch dressing onto her salad. "We won't move far."

"But it's our house!" Bopper wailed. "Daddy wouldn't sell it if he was here!"

Daddy, Karen thought, *is the reason we have to sell it.* But instead of speaking, she kicked off her shoes and ate another chicken nugget. And reminded herself that in the long run, she was getting the better of the deal: sharing in the children's lives, watching them grow up.

"I'm doing the best I can," she told Bopper and, pointing to the little toy that had come with his meal, changed the subject. "Is that an alien or a robot?"

The evening passed quietly. Seven o'clock came and went, and then eight, and still George hadn't shown up. Karen had tucked Bopper into bed and was reading *Peter Pan* to Rose when the bell chimed downstairs.

Startled, Karen checked her watch. An hour and a half late. Whoever this buyer was, already she didn't like him.

Flicking on lights, she walked downstairs and opened the door to admit her boss and a tall, familiar figure.

"Karen." George smiled and stepped inside. "This is Terry Vogel."

No wonder she'd run into him at the shopping center today, Karen realized; he must have just come from meeting with George. It was all very commonplace. A chance meeting, a buyer for her house. So why did she feel as if fate had cut her out of the herd, roped and tied her? She'd left him behind. Now, standing so close, his presence wrapped her in a two-person cocoon.

"Wow," Terry said. "I love this place." But he wasn't looking at the staircase with its polished oak banister or the living room or the lace-curtained dining room. He was staring straight at Karen.

She didn't consider herself anything much to look at: average height, average weight, gray eyes, short light brown hair. How did Terry manage to make her aware all at once of her slender waist and firm breasts, of all the womanly urges she'd suppressed for the past two years?

"May I?" Terry ambled past, peering around corners as if he were opening presents on Christmas. "Look at this little alcove! They don't build houses like this anymore." He strolled through the dining room on impossibly long legs. "And this kitchen! It's like something out of a storybook. Do you really cook with those copper pans?"

"That's what they're for." Despite an undeniable attraction, Karen had to fight the urge to snap at him. She couldn't afford the payments and the maintenance on this place, but the prospect of actually selling it roused her fighting instincts.

"Do you have children, Mr. Vogel?" she heard herself say, when George paused for breath during his sales pitch. "There's a swing set in the backyard."

"Not yet." Terry favored her with a lopsided grin. "May I go upstairs? Your kids aren't asleep yet, are they? I'm sorry to be late. There was an accident on the freeway and I sat there for over an hour."

"Well—sure." She stood back as if he might run over her in a mad rush for the staircase.

Instead, Terry touched her elbow. "You will come up with us, won't you?"

"I'd be happy to show you—" George began.

"But it's her house," Terry explained pleasantly. "She loves it—I could see that at once. You aren't moving very far away, are you?" he asked Karen, and then—without waiting for an answer—added, "She's exactly the woman I hoped to find here. She's perfect."

"I'm afraid she's not for sale," George joked as they climbed to the second floor. "I can't afford to lose a good secretary."

"The master bedroom is over there." Karen pointed, anxious to return to impersonal subjects. "The guest room is there and my daughter's . . ."

"What about the turret?" Terry asked. "Does someone sleep there?"

"My son, Bopper," she said, indicating the curved stairway that led to the third floor.

"May I?" Terry bounded upward with surprising agility for such a tall man. "Oh, hey! Are you Bopper?" His voice drifted down. "You have all those Legos? And a complete set of Transformers. I'm impressed!"

Not wanting to crowd the turret, George and Karen stayed on the second floor. Her boss gave Karen a shrug. "He's a horror novelist and he loves the house because it looks like it should be haunted. It takes all kinds, I guess."

"A horror novelist?" She peered up the staircase and wondered if she should rescue her son. "You mean he writes about disembodied spirits and bloody whatevers?"

"Apparently." George produced a book from beneath his jacket. "He gave me this."

Karen fingered the glossy cover, which featured a painting of a fanged man wearing a baseball uniform. The title was *Major League Vampire*.

"Is this for real?" she asked. Yet she'd already discovered her would-be buyer was a natural storyteller.

Terry skimmed down the stairs. "Fabulous place! But he shouldn't leave the Legos in the bucket—he ought to be building something. It's bad luck."

"I'll remember that," Karen said.

Bopper scampered down after Terry and trailed along as they toured the other rooms. For once, her son had nothing to say, except when he whispered to Karen, "Does he remind you of Tigger?"

"He certainly bounces," she murmured. In the enclosed space, Terry's vibrancy made him seem larger than life. She was acutely aware of how he lifted objects and ran his hand over smooth surfaces. A tactile man, he apparently needed the input of his physical senses.

Remembering how he had touched her shoulder in the parking lot, Karen shivered.

Rose was sitting up in bed when they peered into her room. In her flowered flannel nightgown, with a round-faced doll clutched at her side, she looked like a nineteenth-century figurine.

Terry focused at once on the stack of books next to the bed, the entire *Anne of Green Gables* set. "Have you seen the video?" he asked. "I could lend it to you, if you want to see it."

"Oh, I'd love to!" Rose cried.

"Done," he said.

As they descended to the first floor, leaving the children behind, Terry spoke close to Karen's ear. "I don't mean to pry, but I take it you're a single mom."

"Yes." She swallowed hard as his breath tickled her ear. Karen mistrusted the way his energy vibrated through her. Boyish vulnerability was what had attracted her to Bobby in the first place.

"It's just that—" Terry cleared his throat "—I used to read about Green Gables because I felt as if I were an orphan like Anne. I wondered if Rose—well, forgive me if I'm intruding, but I hope her father isn't dead."

"No such luck." Karen smiled in spite of herself. "I'm sorry. I don't mean to sound bitter."

She might have said more, but George was rubbing his hands together. "Would you care to see the backyard? There's a porch—"

"I've seen enough," Terry said. "Thank you." He took Karen's hand, manipulating the fingers in a motion somewhere between a massage and a caress. "It's a splendid house. You probably bake cookies, don't you?"

"The occasion has arisen." Her throat had taken on a thick lump that made it hard to speak. "It isn't difficult, you know."

"Few things are, if you have the knack." Terry pressed the back of her hand against his cheek absentmindedly. She could feel a hint of roughness. "You've created something wonderful here."

"We refinished the woodwork." She felt foolish, but she didn't know how else to respond. "The previous owners really let it run down."

"I didn't mean the house," Terry said. "A home. You've created a home."

The way he said it tied a knot in Karen's chest. Yes, that was exactly what she'd done. And in a funny way, that was why Bobby had left.

"Mr. Vogel," George said.

"Right." Terry released Karen's hand. "Many thanks for your time."

"My pleasure," she said, meaning it but not wanting to.

After the men left, she wandered through the house. It seemed larger than usual, and her footsteps had a hollow ring. Even the air felt different, chillier, without Terry.

After checking on the children and finding them both drifting into sleep, Karen heated water in a copper kettle and fixed herself a cup of coffee. Sitting at the small rosewood table in the kitchen, she told herself that Terry Vogel probably acted the same way with everybody. Just like Bobby, one of those perpetual charmers.

He wouldn't buy the house, she told herself, and opened the latest issue of *Time* magazine. Despite her efforts to concentrate on world events, she kept seeing a tall, athletic figure striding through her house, changing all the dimensions.

Finally she set the magazine aside and admitted one small truth: that she'd never realized Rose felt like an orphan. How had Terry, who knew nothing about any of them, recognized it instantly?

He was a perceptive man. She'd have to read one of his novels, Karen decided. If she could find the time.

Chapter Two

The lock on the candy shop door slipped easily. The burglar grunted in disgust—he was an old pro who took pride in his work, and he preferred a challenge.

On the other hand, he wasn't in the mood for any more setbacks. That dog in the antique store last night, now that had nearly thrown his pacemaker for a loop. He'd been lucky to get away with nothing worse than a hole in his sock. Make that one more hole in his sock.

The burglar paused in the rear doorway to inhale the mingled scents of chocolate and peppermint with a touch of ginger. He liked to rob old stores, stores with character and a history behind them. It made him feel like Jesse James, instead of one of those drugged-out losers who masqueraded as thieves these days.

The scent took him back to his childhood, when he'd bought candy for a penny right here in the Maycap Candy Emporium, back when Buffalo was a thriving metropolis. Cinnamon twists and candy canes. Made his mouth water to think about it.

The burglar paced quietly to the cash register,

trying not to mind the twinges in his hip. Rainy weather always brought out his arthritis.

It was an old register, easy to get into but empty. That meant they probably kept the money in a cigar box somewhere in the back.

Before going to search, the old man found a red-and-white-striped paper sack and picked out a selection of candies. They had to be soft and gooey. No jawbreakers for him these days.

He was careful not to take too many. Fat burglars didn't last long.

The candy tucked into his shoulder bag and a caramel melting in his mouth, he shuffled to the small office in the back of the store. It wasn't even locked.

When he opened the door, it made a funny squeaking sound, as if it were pinching a mouse. Stale air wafted toward him, as if the door hadn't been opened in a long time.

From inside, the burglar thought he heard a noise. A wet slurping, like a dog panting on a hot day. He froze in the doorway and played his flashlight around the room. Not another dog, please, Lord.

What he saw wasn't a dog. What he saw was something not meant to be hidden in the back of candy stores, or anywhere else on this earth.

What he saw made his pacemaker slam to attention and then fade, fade, fade, as the old man crumpled to the floor.

The Thursday-night critique group sat silent for a moment after Terry finished, and then his friend Joni said, "That's terrific, Terry."

"We can always count on you for a real zinger," added another member.

"Okay, okay." The group's president, Bernice Rule, author of literary short stories and one novel-in-progress, tapped on the table and surveyed the bank meeting room. "Who wants to go first? Mitch?"

Mitch Marakian, writer of popular detective novels, chewed on his pipe and contemplated his notes. "Well, Terry, I like it a lot," he said. "There were a few things—I don't think caramel melts in your mouth."

"Yes, it does," Joni piped up. "Kind of. Until you get to the last little bit, anyway."

Bernice shot her a silencing look.

"And I caught a repetition of 'as if,'" Mitch went on. "'As if it were pinching a mouse,' 'as if it hadn't been opened.' And I'm not sure whether a pacemaker failing would mean instant death."

"I'll check it out." Terry scribbled a reminder on his pad.

"Okay, Joni," Bernice said. "Your turn."

"You have this marvelous way of scaring us and making us laugh at the same time." Joni leaned her bony elbows on the table. "I loved the stuff about fat burglars. I think this book is going to be even bigger than *The Phantom of the Post Office.*"

"Thank you." Terry tried to look modest, although privately he agreed with her.

"What's the title again?" someone asked.

"Tentatively *Dream a Little Scream of Me,*" he said. "I have to make sure it hasn't been used."

"Didn't you say you'd already sold it, on an outline?" Bernice asked.

"Yes, and my editor's already talking a heavy promotion." Terry enjoyed sharing his good news with friends. "By the way, did I mention the actors they're talking about for the film of *Phantom of the Post Office?* Kathleen Turner and Michael Douglas. Of course, they might not be available." Inwardly Terry could clearly see Turner and Douglas filling the big screen with his story.

Other people tended to view him as overly optimistic, he knew, and yet he'd found that confidence usually paid off. When you believed in yourself, other people did, too. It was a trick he'd learned long ago, as a lonely kid who discovered that when he amused his classmates and outraged the grown-ups, he never lacked for friends.

Since then he'd always had plenty of pals, like the dozen writers in this critique group. He'd been a member for five years, starting back when he worked for an advertising agency.

His fellow writers had shredded his first novel, but he'd learned from their comments and gone on to sell three books. Terry wasn't afraid of criticism; it was the only way to improve. At thirty-two, the only thing that could frighten him was the prospect of being locked into a situation he couldn't control.

But he'd never be a kid again, dumped at his grandmother's house in Amherst, Massachusetts, aching to see his father. Never again would he let himself get straitjacketed into a life that chafed against his natural tendencies.

After the rest of his critique group finished commenting, it was Joni Rodd's turn to read. All angles and knobs except for her shock of red-blond hair, Joni reminded Terry of a friendly stork.

Her story was set in a world of elves and princes. Joni hadn't sold a book yet, but she was getting close. She had a deft touch with fantasy and Terry enjoyed her characters.

The group praised her and identified some flaws. Joni captured every comment in agitated shorthand. "Thank you, thank you," she said when they were done. "That's so helpful."

Bernice declared the meeting over. Glancing at the clock, Terry saw that it was only a few minutes past ten.

"Anybody for ice cream?" he asked. Most of the members demurred, citing work the following day, but Mitch and Joni took him up on it. Terry had counted on Mitch accepting; the mystery writer lived alone and was never eager to get home.

Like me, Terry thought, visualizing the cluttered town house he rented. Full though it might be with his pets and miscellany, it felt painfully empty at times. He wouldn't mind leaving it, not a bit.

Joni, who never gained weight, ordered the biggest sundae available at the ice-cream parlor. Mitch passed up ice cream for a glass of sarsaparilla, while Terry had the waitress concoct a special sundae in black and white, licorice and vanilla, mostly because he liked the looks of it.

"You think of such neat things!" Joni declared when their orders were delivered to their fake-marble table. From the next booth, two young women glanced over and whispered to each other.

"I want to see you eat it." Mitch tapped his pipe against the table. He rarely smoked it, just chewed on the end and cultivated a tweedy, professorial image.

"Every bite, Terry. I'll bet you don't even like licorice."

"I'm celebrating." Terry spoiled his creation by slathering it with butterscotch. "I'm buying a house."

"That's great!" Joni said between mouthfuls of ice cream.

"With what?" Mitch eyed him dubiously. "Don't tell me your publisher coughed up an advance to match the big words."

"Well, no." Writing books didn't pay as well as most people assumed, although Terry considered himself on the verge of vast riches. "Actually, Mitch, you're going to loan me the money."

His friend favored him with a raised shaggy eyebrow.

"I had a meeting Monday with my producer," Terry explained. "He expects to pick up the option on *Phantom* and be in production by next summer. Things are coming together. And I've found the perfect house."

"I shudder to think what you consider the perfect house," Mitch said. "As for the movie industry, remember what happened with *my* book."

One of his detective novels had gone through three stars, four directors and finally made it to preproduction, when the studio management changed and all existing projects were dropped.

"Look, I'll have the house for collateral," Terry said. "I can make a twenty-percent down payment. I live frugally. You can't lose."

"My lawyer draws up the paperwork?" Mitch said. "There'll be a balloon payment due in a year, Terry. I don't fool around when it comes to money."

"I don't expect you to," Terry said, delighted. "Thanks, Mitch. This means a lot to me."

"What kind of house is it?" Joni looked up from her ravaged sundae.

Terry launched into a description of the Victorian home, with its appealing nooks, tantalizing crannies and magnificent turret.

The only problem was that although he'd originally visualized himself writing in a tower, he couldn't get that little boy out of his mind. Or that lonely little girl, either.

And he couldn't stop picturing their mother. Karen. She was a lot prettier than anyone's mother had a right to be.

Karen Loesser belonged in that house as much as her children did. Terry felt bad about displacing them, even though he knew another buyer would have come along sooner or later.

"Sounds perfect," Joni said as he finished his description and picked up the check.

"Sounds like you're up to something," Mitch observed. "What precisely was the meaning of that faraway expression, Terry?"

"It's not just going to be my house." Terry shot his friends a smile. "It's going to be my home. If I can keep some special occupants from leaving."

"Speaking of leaving," Joni said, "I've got school tomorrow." She taught second grade, and Terry felt certain the children doted on her.

As they stood up, one of the young women from the next table came over. "Excuse me," she said to Mitch, "aren't you that mystery writer? Mitch Marakian?"

He harrumphed his assent and chewed on his pipe.

"Could I get your autograph?" she asked.

"Glad to." He slid into the next booth, absorbing both women in conversation.

Terry escorted Joni to her car and then loped through the parking lot to his outrageously decorated Volkswagen bug. He'd won a bet with a body-shop owner on the outcome of the World Series, resulting in his car's being turned into a dragon, tail and all.

He checked his watch, saw that it was nearly eleven o'clock, and wondered if it was too late to call the real-estate broker at home to report his decision. Well, why not? It ought to make George happy.

THE DREAM CAME AS KAREN lay halfway between wakefulness and sleep, so she felt as if it actually had happened.

Bopper and Rose were filling the living room with soap bubbles. Colors bounced and twinkled, and Karen began to swirl with them.

Suddenly she was inside one of the globes. Her fingers pressed into a cushioned clear surface, like the bubble wrap used to pack fragile items. She heard faint music, blurred like a neighbor's radio.

Someone pulled her to her feet, swaying inside the sphere. Karen tilted her head back and saw Terry.

"Do you come here often?" He claimed her waist with his arm.

As if she stood outside herself, Karen watched them dancing, two dark figures silhouetted against a sparkly silver world. At the same time, she felt his body moving, his thigh brushing hers, his hand pressing her waist. His cheek grazed her hair as they glided through the waltz like an ethereal Fred Astaire and Ginger Rogers.

His nearness provoked a series of electric tingles along her shoulders and breasts. Their limbs entwined and yet they never stumbled.

She had the sensation that he was making love to her without removing their clothes. It was as if, within the soap bubble, they had melted together.

Karen must have slipped into a dreamless state then, because she was aware of nothing more.

ON THE COMPUTER Karen paged through the Click Art, seeking something suitable for an open-house flier. A shack was definitely out; she didn't much care for a rose-covered cottage, either—not when the property to be advertised was a half-million-dollar pillared monstrosity that looked like a refugee from *Gone with the Wind*.

She settled on a computerized image of a woman in a flowing Roman-style gown, with a wreath of leaves in her hair. "Classic Grandeur," Karen type in large letters.

The door to George's office opened and he ushered out a young couple. "I'll have that list of one-bedroom condos by tomorrow," he promised. "My secretary will get on it right away."

Karen sighed. She had plenty of work piled up already, but there was no point in reminding George.

"Karen!" he said after the clients had gone. "Listen, I've been meaning to talk to you."

"Yes?" She looked up warily.

"That writer wants to make an offer on your house."

Karen's throat clamped shut. She was afraid that if she tried to respond, the only thing to come out would be a pitiful squeak. An offer. Terry Vogel was going to take her house away.

She hoped the offer would be too low. Or that he would win the lottery and decide to buy a mansion in Beverly Hills instead.

"I'll be meeting with him to write it up tomorrow afternoon," George went on, oblivious to her distress. "I thought I might present the offer Saturday night."

Never, Karen reflected, would George consider scheduling it during the hours she worked for him. Not that she expected him to, but it might be a nice touch, especially since he was going to earn a fat commission.

"I can't do it Saturday night," she said. "We're having dinner at my brother's house."

"I promised to take my kids to Knott's Berry Farm on Sunday," George said. "And I have an opening in my schedule tomorrow night at seven."

"No," Karen said.

On the point of arguing, he stopped. Maybe he'd finally remembered that right now she was functioning as a client, not a secretary.

"Very well," George said. "Sunday afternoon okay? Fourish?"

"Four sharp." Karen decided to press her advantage. "I start cooking dinner at five, George."

"Okay." His beeper sounded and he hurried into his office to return the call.

Karen went back to her computer.

When she'd started working for George, it had been on a part-time basis. With a one-year-old and a three-year-old, she'd simply wanted to get out of the house and to keep her job skills current.

Or perhaps she'd had an intuition about Bobby even then. He'd never been happy as an accountant; she couldn't imagine why he'd picked that line of work when he really wanted to be an artist. Knowing Bobby, she guessed he'd chosen something he hated so he'd have a good excuse to give it up.

When he left two years ago, Karen had been grateful for the chance to work full-time. Despite having taken some classes in marketing, she had only a little job experience. And employers didn't exactly go wild about hiring displaced homemakers.

She fought down the familiar wave of dismay sweeping over her. Yes, she was lucky to have a job, but George didn't pay enough for her to keep the house, not without dipping into a small inheritance from her grandmother that was reserved for the kids' education.

Karen wasn't looking forward to the move, but plenty of women relocated their families. She'd find someplace nearby, so Rose wouldn't have to change schools and Marian could still baby-sit, and pretty soon the kids would forget they'd lived in the old Victorian.

Kids had short memories. A lot shorter than Karen's.

AT SIX-THIRTY on Saturday morning, a velour bathrobe wrapped tightly around her, Karen darted outside to retrieve the newspaper.

This was her secret time, before the kids awakened. At this hour, the house lay quiet and the entire neighborhood still slumbered. It was her time to indulge in coffee, home-baked blueberry muffins and silence.

It made Karen wonder why she'd been in such a hurry to get married so young. Sure, she'd wanted children, and she'd felt keenly the need for a man around the house after losing her father early. But she'd missed having a chance to live alone and get to know her own life rhythms.

At least she was blessed with children who slumbered late on weekends, giving her the healing gift of solitude, Karen reminded herself as she hurried out the door.

Only on this particular Saturday, things didn't go according to plan.

For one thing, the temperature had dropped near freezing the previous night, and cold air nipped at Karen's bare ankles above her slippers. Gusts of wind tugged at her bathrobe, parting it to reveal the lacy wisp of a nightgown beneath.

But the biggest problem was that as Karen emerged from the porch and ran down the walkway, Terry Vogel snapped her picture.

"What?" Astonished, she stopped stock-still and tugged her bathrobe shut.

"I beg your pardon." He looked startled. "I was taking some pictures of the house. I hope you don't mind."

Karen tried not to notice the appealing picture he made, his cheeks pink from the cold and his blue eyes glittering above a colorful ski sweater. Gorgeous or not, he had no right to be here.

"I do mind!" She snatched up the newspaper. "This is still my house, and I'm entitled to some privacy!"

"I wasn't expecting you in the shot," Terry explained. "You ran in front of me."

He sounded so reasonable, Karen had to force herself not to back down. "It's six-thirty in the morning!"

"Six-forty-five." Terry covered the lens on his camera. "Would you like me to burn the negative? That's a very pretty bathrobe."

He was maneuvering her out of her bad mood, and Karen wasn't ready to give it up. "George hasn't even presented your offer yet."

"I know. I can still talk to you, can't I?" Terry followed as Karen, her face smarting from the cold, started back for the house.

"If you like." His presence disturbed her in more ways than one. Retreating into the welcome warmth of the living room, Karen wondered how she was going to get rid of Terry without slamming the door in his face. "I was going to read the paper."

"Don't let me stop you." He stepped inside and closed the door against the cold air. Indoors, he seemed larger and his shoulders broader. His mouth, quirking with a hint of a smile, came much too close to hers.

"Is that the scent of—" he said.

"Do you want some—" she began. They stopped. Her breathing sounded abnormally loud in her own ears. He was *much* too close.

"Does it matter what we say?" He eased toward her. "We could both talk at the same time, or we could say nothing at all."

"What?" Karen fought the urge to back away, and then realized she didn't really want to.

He fingered her shoulder, tracing the delicate bones beneath the fabric, and her entire body quivered in response. She hadn't felt this way since . . . ever.

"I feel as if we're having a conversation," Terry said. "Without speaking. This is new to me. You, too?"

She nodded stiffly, and then realized she'd made a dangerous concession. "I mean—I don't know what— you're a writer. You imagine things."

"Do I?" He leaned forward as if to brush his lips over hers, and Karen tensed beneath a shiver of panic.

She didn't want this, not now, and especially not from him.

Terry's eyes bored into hers, holding her motionless, and then he nodded to himself. "Those muffins I smell *are* blueberry, aren't they?"

"Yes." The tension drained out of Karen's shoulders.

"Good," Terry said. "Blueberry's my favorite."

She led the way through the house. "Do you want coffee?"

"Yes, please. Black." As he folded himself into a kitchen chair, Terry added, "You don't trust me, do you?"

"Nothing personal." Karen transferred a muffin to a plate and handed him a cup of coffee. "I'd hate anyone who bought my house."

"I see." Terry regarded her thoughtfully. "That's all? I wonder." He tasted the muffin. "This is great. You baked it yourself?"

"From a mix." Karen set the newspaper aside. She needed to keep her wits about her with Terry sitting so close, his long legs accidentally grazing hers from time to time.

"I tried a mix once," he said. "Did you make the kind with the can of blueberries in the box? How do you keep from eating all the dough?"

"You have a disconcerting habit," she countered, "of asking a second question before the first one's been answered."

"It comes from not having my questions answered when I was small," Terry said. "My grandmother believed children should be seen and not . . . heard."

His words trailed off with the appearance in the doorway of two rumpled figures. Rose regarded him

solemnly above the doll she snuggled to her chest, while
Bopper shuffled in trailing his favorite blanket.

"Did you buy our house?" the little boy demanded,
sliding into his seat. "Are we moving?"

"Not yet." Karen set out their muffins and milk.
"Terry's just visiting."

"You shouldn't come here," Rose told him, not
stirring from the doorway. "People might think you're
going to kick us out."

"You guys don't sound too eager to sell." Terry
pushed Bopper's chair up to the table. "Why are you,
if you don't mind my asking?"

"Because Daddy went away." Rose perched on the
edge of her seat and propped her doll beside the plate.
"Mommy doesn't make enough money. Do you make
lots of money?"

"Sometimes," Terry said. "I've sold one of my
books to the movies. That means actors and actresses
are going to pretend to be my characters, and they pay
me well for the privilege. But I won't buy your house
if you don't want me to."

"I wish we had lots of money," Bopper said. "I'd
get a radio-controlled car and a huge electric-train set.
Daddy's going to get them for me when he comes
back."

"No, he won't." Rose cut her muffin into quarters.

"He will, too." Bopper crammed his whole muffin
into his mouth at once and choked.

"Bopper?" Karen whacked him on the back.
"Bopper!" A wad of muffin flew out of the boy's
mouth.

Terry handed him a glass of milk. "Drink this!"

Spluttering, Bopper downed the milk. His breathing returned to normal.

"Are you all right?" Karen hugged the little boy. She skated close to hysteria these days, she realized. It wasn't the first time Bopper had choked after eating and talking at the same time, but she felt vulnerable right now, as if losing her house meant she might lose her family, too.

"I'm done eating," Bopper said calmly. "I want to go out and play, Mommy." He wiggled from her grasp and ran out of the room.

Rose pushed her plate away. "I'd better make sure he puts his coat on." She regarded Terry. "I guess if somebody has to buy our house, I'm glad it's you."

"Oh!" He reached into his camera bag and pulled out a videotape. "*Anne of Green Gables*, as promised."

The girl accepted the tape with great care. "Can I watch this today, Mom?"

"While Bopper takes his nap," Karen promised.

Rose walked quietly from the room.

"I worry about them," Karen said, before she remembered who she was talking to. "But we'll be fine, as soon as we get settled."

Terry stood up. "You're still shaking."

"I'm fine." She cleared her throat as she arose. "Really."

He touched her elbow. She felt supported, as if she were leaning on him. "I don't know how a man could leave those children," he said. "And you."

"You don't know Bobby." Karen began scraping the dishes. "He never really grew up. One day he got a letter from an old college friend, inviting him to join an artists' colony in Oregon, and bam, he left. Gave me a week's notice, after six years of marriage and two kids.

Although, to be fair, I knew he felt frustrated sometimes. 'Unfulfilled' was the word he used.''

Terry ran hot water into the sink and poured in some detergent. "He made his choices and left you to take the consequences."

"You're a writer," Karen pointed out. "I should think you'd sympathize with him."

"I do." Terry scrubbed the muffin pan. "With his need to create art. But—"

The rear screen door slammed as the kids raced outside. From the yard came Bopper's shouts as he headed for the swing set. "What are you going to do with this big house, all by yourself?" Karen asked.

Terry's face grew solemn as he rinsed a coffee cup. "I hope I won't have it all to myself for long."

"Girlfriend?" Karen asked.

"Not yet."

"I envy you," she said. "Starting fresh, no painful memories. Or are there?"

"I was engaged once." Terry stacked clean dishes in the drainer. "Couple of years ago. Her name was Francie. Blond hair, long legs, but I think what I liked best was her kid. She had this little girl named Dreamy. Can you imagine naming a child Dreamy? Bopper's a nickname, isn't it?"

"For Bob, Jr.," Karen agreed, trying to keep up with his train of thought. "What happened to Francie?"

Terry leaned against the counter. "We had fun together but she wasn't ready to settle down, which I suppose was a good thing for me, as it turned out. Francie went to Africa with some vague idea about doing missionary work and ended up marrying a Zulu prince. At least, she said he was a prince, and who am I to doubt it?"

"Did it hurt when she left?" Karen wondered what made her ask such a personal question. "When Bobby went, I felt betrayed. Angry and hurt and bitter. I guess I still do, although I'm trying to get past it."

"Francie didn't hurt me," Terry acknowledged. "I guess that's when I realized I hadn't been in love. I just wanted a family and it was fun going places with her and Dreamy."

"I'm glad you're the one who's going to have this house." Karen picked up a towel to dry the dishes. "You'll fill it with happiness, and that's the way it should be." She turned aside, hoping he wouldn't notice the catch in her voice.

Gentle hands skimmed her shoulders. "Karen?" Terry's breath whispered across her neck. "I don't have to buy it. Stay here, if it means so much."

"It's only a house." Karen pulled back and faced him. "I won't use the money my grandmother left for Rose and Bopper. No house is worth that."

"But you belong here," he said.

"Don't you think I know that?" she cried. "I don't need you to point out . . . I'm sorry."

"I'm the one who's sorry." He made no move to touch her again. "I'm butting in where I have no business. My specialty."

Karen shrugged. "Sometimes I'm too touchy. Thanks for washing the dishes."

"If you like, I could wait while you get dressed," Terry said. "We could play ball with Bopper."

He sounded so wistful that Karen nearly gave in, but she restrained the urge. "I think it would be better if you left. The kids and I are going through a difficult time right now. We aren't ready to make new friends,

especially someone who's going to take our house.
Even though we need to sell it.''

Deep in those blue eyes, she caught a glimpse of
sadness. ''There wouldn't be any harm in my bringing
the kids Christmas presents, would there?''

''Not in moderation.'' If he'd made so much money
on his movie deal that he could afford to buy the house
outright, he might do something foolishly extrava-
gant. ''Nothing too expensive, Terry.''

''I promise.'' He grinned. ''It's more fun selecting
lots of little things, anyway.''

''Lots?'' Karen said. ''Wait a minute...''

''See you!'' Terry called over his shoulder as he
bounded toward the living room. Like Tigger, Karen
conceded silently—Bopper had been right. ''Thanks
for breakfast!''

''Burn the negative!'' she called, but her words were
lost in the click of the front door closing.

Chapter Three

"Oh, Good! He didn't make you work this week-end!" Marian Joseph opened the front door to admit Karen, her children and the dish of cream-cheese enchiladas that Rose had helped prepare.

Marian, wearing a flowing Hawaiian-style hostess gown, had tucked a white carnation into her long, curly hair. Although only twenty-three, she seemed ageless, a natural earth mother who took wonderful care of Karen's brother, Sid, and their three-year-old daughter, Lisa.

The two women embraced. They'd become instant friends when they first met, and after Bobby left, Marian had proved a lifesaver.

"He tried to make me work, but I put my foot down." Karen wasn't ready to confess the painful truth, that her boss was spending the afternoon writing an offer on her own house.

Stepping inside, she inhaled the scent of saffron rice and apple pie, two of her sister-in-law's specialties. "Is Mom here yet?"

"Sid's picking her up. He had to haul a load to Santa Barbara so he can swing by West LA on the way back."

Marian waved toward the overstuffed den. "Lisa is watching *The Rescuers Down Under.*"

"Let's go!" Bopper raced in that direction. Rose hesitated as if debating whether to join the grown-ups, then trailed in her brother's wake.

"What did parents ever do before video?" Karen accompanied her sister-in-law into the dining room.

"Died young."

The Josephs' wood-frame house formed a marked contrast to her own home two blocks away. Slapped together in the fifties during one of Whittier's growth spurts, it lacked any architectural pretensions. Cheap wood paneling covered parts of the interior walls, while the floor disappeared beneath shag carpeting. An overabundance of furniture made the rooms look even smaller than they were, yet Karen felt comfortable here.

Terry's words came to mind. A home. She and Marian both seemed able to create them. You wouldn't think a horror novelist such as Terry Vogel would care about something like that.

"Your mother..." Marian checked to make sure no little ears were listening. "I adore her, but, honestly, how can anyone live in Southern California and not drive? Especially after she moved to West Los Angeles." It was almost forty miles from Whittier.

"It's easy when your son's a truck driver," Karen pointed out. "If Sid would stop picking her up, maybe she'd have to get her license."

"He couldn't do that." Marian popped into the kitchen to stir the rice, and Karen followed. "You know your Mom. Someone will always take care of her."

For a long time, that someone had been Karen. Helene Joseph had been widowed in her late thirties, left with a sixteen-year-old daughter, an eleven-year-old son and a modest amount of insurance money.

It was Karen who'd taken over most of their father's responsibilities, running interference with repairmen, chauffeuring her mother to the grocery store, filling out their income-tax forms. Karen had also worked after school and on weekends to help make ends meet.

Yet she'd never resented her role. Helene had done her best at a seemingly endless series of clerking and sales jobs, and she was a wonderful cook. Somehow the bills always got paid.

Karen missed her mother since Helene had moved back to the area where she'd grown up. She had a lot of friends there from church and the garden club.

Helene had the gift of contentment—pleasure in simple things, joy in her grandchildren, a ready acceptance of whatever life brought. Karen hoped that someday she too could find such serenity.

"Karen," Marian said. "There's something I wanted to talk to you about..." She stopped at the sound of the front door opening. "Later."

Bustle and chatter filled the house as the children tumbled out to greet their grandmother.

At dinner, Helene regaled them with stories of the latest church fair, and Sid, a bluff, good-natured young man, teased her about her new hairstyle. The permanent might be a bit too curly, Karen decided, but it softened her mother's features.

It made Helene look younger. Although in her fifties, she had sometimes seemed a decade older. Not anymore. Was there, Karen wondered, such a thing as a second wind in life as well as in exercise?

Afterward, Karen and Marian retreated with the dishes while everyone else stretched out to watch the evening news.

"Good, we're alone." Marian plunged her hands into soapy water. "Karen, I had a call from Bobby."

It took all Karen's concentration not to spill the rice she was scooping into a plastic storage container. "Oh?"

"He asked about the children." Marian watched her reaction sympathetically. "He said he wanted to be sure they were getting along okay, but he didn't want to disturb you."

"Disturb me!" Karen snapped the lid onto the container. "He doesn't want to be hounded for child support, that's what. Marian, I know he doesn't have an income. I just want him to talk to Bopper and Rose. They're hurting so badly."

"He doesn't want to deal with it," her sister-in-law observed. "He doesn't like to face what he's done to them."

Karen tore a sheet of aluminum foil to store leftover pie. "I don't suppose he mentioned Christmas."

"Avoided the subject like the plague."

Karen crimped the foil with such ferocity that she tore it. "Isn't it ironic? Some fathers fight for custody. My ex won't even talk to his kids on the phone. How did I ever marry such a jerk?"

"Bobby can be charming when he wants to be," Marian reminded her.

Terry Vogel could be charming, too, although he didn't seem wrapped up in himself like Bobby. But Terry was going to take away her home.

To her horror, Karen began to cry. It started as a small trickle and then she was leaning on her sister-in-law's shoulder, sobbing.

"It's okay," Marian murmured. "You're entitled."

"Oh, Marian!" Karen wailed. "George found a buyer! We're going to have to move."

"A nice family?" Marian asked. "People who'll appreciate it?"

"A horror novelist!" Karen cried. "Oh, Marian, he's going to take my house!"

"The dirty rat," her sister-in-law said.

In spite of herself, Karen began to smile. And then laughter swelled up, so long and deep that she had to sit down to keep from losing her balance.

"It wasn't that funny," Marian said drily.

"Yes, it was!" Karen gasped. "It's ridiculous, isn't it? Here I've been complaining about pouring every cent into the house. And now someone comes along to take it off my hands and I hate him, I positively hate him."

"What kind of horror novels?" Marian asked. "It isn't Stephen King, is it?"

"Hardly." Karen resumed putting away the leftovers. "Ever hear of a book called *Major League Vampire?*"

"You mean Terry Vogel?" Marian demanded. "Terry Vogel is buying your house?"

"You've heard of him?" Karen searched through the refrigerator to find room for a packet of ham.

"He's hilarious." Her sister-in-law sprayed rinse water across a plate. "Could I get his autograph?"

"Traitor!" Karen said.

"What's he like in person?"

The adjectives that came to mind, oddly, were all flattering. "Full of energy. Impressed with everything. Loves kids. He thinks the house ought to be haunted."

"I read somewhere that he's single," Marian said. "Let's see—intelligent, artistic, unattached. Just think—"

Karen wrung water out of a sponge and mopped the table. "As far as I'm concerned, Terry Vogel might as well be sixty years old and wear his clothes inside out."

"What color are his eyes?"

"Blue," Karen said without thinking.

"Hair?"

"Black."

"How tall?"

"Over six feet," she said. "Why?"

"You noticed." Marian smiled. "Watch out."

"If I never see him again, that will be fine with me." Karen rinsed off the sponge.

But as she followed Marian into the living room to join the others, it struck Karen that she didn't know what color George's eyes were, even though she'd worked for him for four years.

So what? Terry Vogel had shocking blue eyes. Very bright and unusual.

Anybody would notice them, Karen told herself firmly. Anyone at all.

"DO TREES HAVE FEELINGS?" Bopper asked as they climbed out of the car. "Do you suppose it minds being tied up like that?"

About to remind him that there had been no other way to fit the pine into the back of her station wagon, Karen checked herself. "I'm sure it's delighted that it's going to be a Christmas tree with an angel on the top and all those bright lights.''

Bopper hopped up and down. "And my wooden soldiers and Rose's pink balls.''

"Oh, Mom,'' Rose said. "Trees don't care about stuff like that. Besides, it's dead.''

"It's not dead!'' Bopper protested as Karen began tugging the tree out the tailgate. "It isn't!''

"I'm not sure I can carry this.'' Karen wondered why it had looked so easy for the man at the Christmas-tree lot. Probably because he was at least six inches taller than she was and about ten years younger. "Rose, would you see if Mr. Rivers is home next door? Maybe he could help us.''

"They went skiing, remember?'' her daughter said. "Mom, could we go to the mountains? Bopper's never seen snow.''

"Next year.'' Karen's efforts to shift the tree onto her shoulders yielded a shower of pine needles. Even without looking, she knew they were clinging to her hair and sweater. "Maybe I should call your Uncle Sid.''

She broke off as the blast of a novelty car horn echoed down the street. *A-ooga, a-ooga!*

"Wow!'' cried Bopper. "Look at that!''

The vehicle tooling toward them must once, Karen supposed, have been an ordinary Volkswagen bug. Some joker had built up a green fiberglass face on the front, an arching scaled body across the top and a tail that wound around the rear bumper.

"It's a dragon!'' Rose said. "Look, Mom!''

"Very nice.'' Karen tried to balance the tree, but she couldn't get the right angle on it. "Rose, take the keys out of my purse, go inside and call Uncle Sid.''

The strange car pulled to the curb. Rose started back in alarm and Bopper grabbed Karen's hand.

The driver's door opened and Terry bounced out. "Do you like it?" he called. "Anybody want a ride?"

"Pleeeeeze, Mommy!" came an immediate chorus.

Karen glared at Terry from beneath the tree. "We're busy."

"So I see." Striding across the driveway, he hefted the tree with ridiculous ease and carted it up the walk. Karen had to hustle to get the front door open fast enough.

He'd caught her off guard again, she realized as she directed Terry to the water-filled tree stand she'd prepared earlier. She wasn't braced for his ebullience, since she hadn't expected to see him again until the final walk-through.

There'd been no choice but to accept his full-price offer two weeks ago, especially as he didn't insist she repaint the house or replace the cracked kitchen linoleum. Since he wouldn't need a bank loan, he'd even agreed to a thirty-day escrow.

Two more weeks and Karen could get her family resettled in the duplex unit she'd rented three blocks away. It might seem cramped, but they'd be close to Sid and Marian's house and Rose wouldn't have to change schools. Best of all, the rent was low enough that Karen wouldn't have to stretch each paycheck to the breaking point.

These past two weeks she'd kept so busy packing and planning that she'd forgotten to prepare herself for Terry's inevitable reappearance. At least it seemed inevitable, now that he was here.

"Is that straight?"

"Perfect." Karen reached to help him steady the trunk. In the moment before he released it, she felt his energy vibrating through the wood and into her arm, as if they'd completed an electrical circuit.

"Have you got it?" His deep voice rumbled into her ear.

"I—I think so."

Terry knelt and tightened the screws. "It's a beautiful tree. You have a good eye."

"It's not beautiful yet," Rose told him. "Wait till you see the globes."

"Globes?" he quirked an eyebrow as he stood up.

"Rose-colored," the little girl said.

"In her honor. They're in the attic." Karen brushed pine needles off her sweater. "We didn't have a tree last year. I guess none of us was up to it, with Bobby gone."

"There's an attic?" Terry said. "Better and better. Which way?"

He'd bought the house without even knowing about the attic, Karen reflected, with a shake of the head, as she led her little troop upstairs.

The attic was reachable via a pull-down ladder. Terry clambered up and began poking around. "I'm sorry," he called down, "all I see is a lot of insulation."

"I'm sure they're up there," Karen responded. "A big cardboard box marked 'ornaments.'"

Terry reappeared in the opening. "Look for yourself."

"They have to be..." Karen stopped midsentence. "Oh, no."

"What, Mommy?" There was an uneasy note in Bopper's voice.

"They've got to be somewhere," Rose said. "It wouldn't be Christmas without Bopper's toy soldiers and my globes."

Stricken, Karen stared at Terry as he climbed down. "I blocked it from my mind. I'm so sorry."

"Breathe deeply," he said. "You look pale. Is this a really awful tragedy, like the kind you call the fire department for, or just sort of painful, like papercuts?"

"I think you'd better call out the National Guard." Karen put her arms around Rose and Bopper. "Kids, do you remember a screaming, howling fight Daddy and I had right before he left?"

Bopper shook his head. Rose frowned. "It was about some collage he made. That great big one he lashed on top of his car when he left."

"The one you never saw," Karen said. "It was called 'Christmas Shattered.'"

Terry stared at her in disbelief. "He didn't."

"He said it was a meaningful act of—what was his word—'disencumberment,'" Karen recalled. "Breaking free of his burdens. He wanted to impress his fellow colonists with his brilliant insight. To me it looked like a mess, a lot of broken pink glass and..." She stopped at the horrified look on Rose's face. "Oh, honey, I'm sorry."

"Daddy broke my ornaments?" The little voice came out thin and tight.

"It was—art." Why, oh, why, hadn't Karen remembered in time? "We'll get some more, Rose."

"I don't want any more." Tears trickled down the girl's cheeks. "Daddy bought those ornaments for me."

"He broke the toy soldiers, too?" Bopper's voice filled with disgust. "I hate him! Can I use some bad words, Mommy? Just this once?"

"No bad words, and it's no use hating Daddy," Karen said briskly. "He didn't mean to hurt you guys. He's immature, that's all. We'll buy some new ornaments, even better."

Her daughter stood firm. "I don't want a Christmas tree. Take it back."

"The best kind of ornaments," Terry said, "are the kind you eat when Christmas is over."

Recognizing a brilliant idea when she heard one, Karen joined in. "I have a recipe for popcorn balls. And Rose, we've got those candy canes you were going to distribute in class. I'll buy some more."

"I'll bet your Mom could figure out a way to make cookies shaped like bells," Terry went on. "And we wouldn't have to use *all* of them on the tree."

"Cookies!" The only thing Bopper liked better was ice cream, and not by much.

"We have to have a tree," Terry pointed out. "I've got a bunch of presents for you guys in my car, and if I don't have a tree to put them under, I'll have to take them back."

"Oh." The little girl chewed on her lower lip. "Well, I guess it would be all right."

Over the children's heads, Karen mouthed the words, "Thank you."

"Think nothing of it." Terry's eyes met hers. "I like cookies, too."

Within half an hour, the house was filled with the fragrance of baked goodies. In a funny way, Karen reflected as she cut the dough with a cookie cutter, she was glad they didn't have the old ornaments that reminded her of Bobby. This was much more fun.

The only problem was Terry, who really did have trouble restraining himself from eating all the dough. Karen swatted him for the third time. "Why don't you go upstairs and do something useful, like build Legos with Bopper?" she asked.

Terry looked as if he might argue, then nodded. "Useful," he said, and vanished.

"Mommy, this batch is done." Karen hurried to help as Rose removed a tray from the oven.

It wasn't for another half hour, until the baking was done and she discovered Bopper asleep in the living room, that she thought to check on Terry.

She wouldn't put it past him to play with blocks by himself, Karen reflected as she mounted the steps to the second floor. She stopped at the distant sound of hammering.

"Terry?" She neared the staircase leading to the tower. "What are you doing?"

"This toy chest was falling apart," came his muffled voice. "I'll be right down."

When Terry lowered himself, he carried a tool kit Bobby had left. The instruments in it were practically new, since Bobby hadn't been handy.

"I've got the knobs back on Rose's dresser, too," Terry informed her. "You'll find the leak is fixed in the bathroom."

"You didn't need to—I mean—"

"No need to thank me. You've been working as hard as I have." He set the took kit on a small table. "I would appreciate a Band-Aid, though, if you have one."

"You're hurt!" Karen took his hand, noticing how drops of blood welled from a cut on the thumb. "I'll get the disinfectant."

"Really, I don't need—"

Her mothering instincts took over as she fetched the appropriate items and began cleaning the cut. "Does that hurt? How'd you do it? I'm so sorry."

"Karen." Terry brushed aside the overgrown bangs that fell in her eyes. "I won't die."

"But it must hurt." She looked up and found him gazing at her. A glow spread across Karen's skin and she felt the heat of his body radiating through his soft cotton shirt. "It's a deep cut."

"I've known deeper ones." With his free hand, he rescued the Band-Aid from her suddenly numb fingers, and applied it himself. "I don't need to be taken care of. What I need from you is—" In midsentence, his mouth closed over hers.

A tingling sensation started at Karen's lips and flowed across her cheeks and nose, down her throat and directly to her breasts and abdomen. She knew she ought to resist, but the pleasure was too great; she hadn't responded to a man in a long time. And even with Bobby, there had never been this sense of a fire building. Of an explosion that any moment might blow her self-control into shards.

When Terry released her, Karen took a moment to pull herself together. "We ought—the children might—"

"I'm sorry," Terry said. "No, amend that. I'm not sorry at all, but I feel I should apologize."

"I don't suppose it really meant anything," Karen managed to say, more for her own benefit than his. "People get carried away sometimes."

"It was very bold of me." Terry sighed. "Especially as I have a favor to ask."

"Yes?"

"The lease on my apartment is up on Monday," Terry said. "I thought it ran through the end of the year, but...well, rather than have to move into a motel for two weeks, I wondered if I could rent your spare room."

How on earth was she going to get out of this? She couldn't have him living across the hall from her bedroom, not for two weeks. Not even for two days.

"The other thing," Terry went on, "is that I'm not sure I can find a motel that will take my pets."

"Pets, plural?" Karen muttered. "Are they housebroken?"

"Not exactly," Terry said. "It's hard to housebreak a chinchilla. Phil, I could board out, but his wife, Gloompuss, is expecting—or at least I think so. It's hard to tell, because she's twice as big as Phil, even under normal circumstances."

"I don't think..."

"They'd be very cozy in the laundry room," Terry said. "Then you'd have me around to help take the tree down, carry boxes and things, help you pack. Plus I'll pay rent, of course. Is three hundred dollars enough?"

"For two weeks? That's too much," Karen said.

"Two hundred and fifty dollars, then." Terry turned away before she could stop him. "Great. Thank you, Karen. You won't regret it."

"Wait..." She was talking to empty air. Terry had already skipped halfway down the stairs and was calling his news to the children.

Chapter Four

Marian held up a pair of crystal salt- and pepper-shakers, a wedding present that Karen had tucked away in her sideboard and never used. "You'll want them later," she said.

They were sitting on the dining-room floor, amid a pile of boxes and oversize sheets of blank newsprint. With only two weeks to go before they moved, Karen had set Saturday afternoon aside for packing.

She studied the shakers in a blur of confusion. She and her sister-in-law had been working for two hours now. At first Karen had set aside the Goodwill donations with ruthless efficiency, but as time went on she'd become less sure of what her future self might want.

"Okay," she said at last. "They're small."

"You need a break, and so do I." Marian stretched and went to check the family room. From the murmurs of childish voices, Karen gathered that Rose, Bopper and Lisa were happily playing.

As Karen made her way to the kitchen to make some coffee, she wondered how they'd adapt to the duplex she'd rented. The unit was only three blocks away, a perfect location, and it shared a small yard where the children could play.

Still, it had only two bedrooms, so Bopper and Rose would have to share. Rents had skyrocketed over the past few years, she'd discovered, and renting a three-bedroom house or apartment would cost almost as much as her present mortgage payments.

There was no family room, and the living room would be crowded with all their furniture. She planned to get rid of some old couches and tables, but she couldn't part with the handsome antique sofa she'd recovered herself, or the magnificent sideboard with its etched-glass windows, or the entertainment center that presently dominated the den.

Karen was in the kitchen, measuring coffee into a filter, when she heard the doorbell. "Marian, could you get that?"

"Sure." Footsteps, a door opening, and then shrieks of delight from the children.

For one heart-sinking moment, she thought it might be Bobby. It would be just like him to pop in now and make her feel even worse about the move.

Then she heard the rumble of a masculine bass voice. Terry! How could she have forgotten he was moving in this weekend?

How could she feel such excitement, such anticipation, when a major chapter in her life was ending? How was she going to get through the next two weeks, the thousand and one tasks she had to accomplish, the children's roller-coaster emotions, while trying to squelch her own response to Terry?

Hearing him now, chatting merrily with her sister-in-law, Karen felt a mellow warmth seep into her bone marrow, felt electricity buzz along her nerve endings, became sharply aware of the masculine scent of cedar....

Cedar?

Karen plopped the filter into place, dumped in the water and hurried to see what was going on.

Her first impression was that the Martians had landed. Or that K mart had decided to hold a sidewalk sale in her living room.

The door had nearly disappeared behind a pile of strapped-together suitcases, oddly shaped cartons and, sitting atop the heap, a large metal cage in which two furry gray shapes bounced across aromatic cedar chips.

Terry stood next to a graying man in a tweed jacket who had his teeth clamped over an unlit pipe and a tall, knobby woman with an eager face.

Terry had roommates? Oh, no.

As if reading her thoughts, he said, "These are some friends from my writers' group. They're helping me move. Karen, meet Mitch Marakian and Joni Rodd."

"You're all writers?" Marian bubbled. "Mitch Marakian! I've read your books! Oh, my. Should I ask for your autograph? No—my manners. We've got cookies in the other room!" She hustled off.

Karen tried not to show her dismay at the pile of oddments invading her living room. This was Terry's home now, too. She hadn't really expected the place to look exactly the same with a new owner, had she?

"I've cleared out the guest room upstairs," she said. "Except for the furniture..."

"Good, because I haven't got any." He touched her shoulders and for some odd reason the gesture brought to mind a magician lulling his subject into hypnosis. That was as good an explanation as any for why Karen stood there amid the clutter and bustle, simply looking back into Terry's eyes. "No furniture except for my rowing machine. Just miscellany and paraphernalia."

"Damned stuff," Mitch said. He glanced at the children's openmouthed reactions and said, "Excuse me. I'm a crusty old bachelor."

Karen swallowed hard, knowing she couldn't simply stand here breathing in Terry's warmth and feeling his hands burn through her shoulders. "Let's ... see if we can't figure out where to put everything."

During the next hour, matters managed to sort themselves out. Boxes were moved upstairs, the children played with the chinchillas, and quantities of coffee and cookies disappeared. At last Rose and Bopper retreated to their rooms, under protest, for their afternoon quiet time.

"They're so cute!" Joni said. "Rose is really bright. I wish I taught locally rather than over in La Mirada. I'd love to have her in my class."

"Thank you." Karen had accepted Joni's offer to help wrap teacups in the kitchen. She wasn't going to pack up everything yet, but it amazed her how much she'd accumulated in eight years.

She set aside a mismatched saucer—where had that come from, anyway?—and wondered for a fleeting moment about Joni's relationship with Terry. He treated his fellow writer with casual camaraderie, but did Joni feel the same way?

"Terry would have made a great teacher," Joni chatted on. "He's marvelous with kids. But he's got too much energy to stay in one place very long. I think he'd burst out the windows of a classroom. A big house like this, it's perfect."

Karen sensed nothing but easy friendship on Joni's part. It spoke well for Terry that he could be pals with a woman. Half an hour later, when Joni departed, Karen waved goodbye with genuine regret.

The house echoed with silence. Marian, Lisa and Mitch had departed earlier; Karen could feel their absence.

It was hard to remember that in two more weeks this house and these new people would be out of her life. No fair holding on. She couldn't let herself find excuses to visit Terry and his friends—for the children's sake, she had to make a clean break with the past.

"You look like someone just walked over your grave," Terry said.

Karen jerked out of her reverie. "What an expression!"

"Comes naturally to a horror novelist."

She led the way to the kitchen, stopped, and eyed the remaining stacks of dishes blearily.

Terry began sticking the dishes back into a cupboard. "I'm done. Are you done? Let the rest of the packing wait till after Christmas. Then I'll help you."

"Well..." Karen's gaze stopped at the chinchilla cage sitting on the table. "Oh, dear."

"Unhygienic." Terry swept it off to the laundry room. "I really do think Gloompuss is pregnant."

Following along, Karen realized that a response would be superfluous. Instead, she took a good look at the chinchillas for the first time.

Phil was about the size of a chipmunk and Gloompuss, as Terry had warned, was nearly twice as big. They had the softest, fluffiest fur she'd ever seen, only they hopped about with the twitchiness of squirrels.

"They're nearly extinct in their native Andes," Terry informed her as he filled a water bottle. "They survive mainly on chinchilla ranches. Can you imagine how many chinchillas it takes to make one coat? I can't stand it. One of life's paradoxes. Fur ranchers keep the species alive, and yet—I saw one of them once at the opera, in L.A. A chinchilla coat. I think it was *Madama Butterfly*. The whole time the diva was singing 'Un Bel Di,' I kept hearing the squeaks of chinchillas." He adjusted the cage atop an old laundry cart. "So here we are."

"Chinchillas and teacups." Karen shook her head.

The next thing she knew, she was being lifted and carried toward the kitchen.

"What—?" she gasped, all too aware of the strength of Terry's arms supporting her. Her cheek, pressed against his T-shirt, registered the powerful thud of his heart.

"We have to do this right." He angled her over the threshold into the kitchen. "Isn't that the tradition?"

"That's for brides," Karen pointed out. "Besides, I'm moving out, not in."

"You never know." Terry seemed in no hurry to put her down. And Karen discovered she was in no hurry, either. Resting against him she felt safe and protected.

"This is nice," she said.

"Uh . . ." He tried to stifle a small grunt, but not before Karen realized that slim as she was, she could hardly be classed as feather-light.

"Maybe you'd better put me down," she suggested.

"I guess so." He deposited her carefully onto a chair. "If you insist." A deep breath rushed out of him. "That was fun. Let's do it again sometime."

"Mommy." Bopper's small voice came from the doorway. "I'm ready for my snack."

"Snack! After all those cookies?" Karen chided as she reached into the refrigerator for a bowl of fruit. "Well, just this once."

BACKING OUT OF the garage had always been something of an adventure, due to the potholes that bloomed unmended in the driveway. They were one of those things Karen could never quite afford to repair.

On this particular Sunday, however, her aging Firebird hit the potholes with a resounding *thump!* that boded even less well than usual. Had the holes really expanded since yesterday?

"Whee!" cried Bopper. "Do it again, Mommy!"

"I think you scraped the bumper," Rose said.

Karen swung out of the car with a sinking feeling. They were on their way to a pre-Christmas dinner with her mother, who was going out of town over the holidays with a group of friends. It was a long drive to Helene's home, and Karen had no desire to get stuck along the freeway.

A quick glance confirmed her fears. One of her tires had gone flat.

Karen leaned against the door frame, weighing options. Her spare tire was the kind that had to be inflated with a special canister, for emergency use only, and it wasn't likely she'd find a tire store open today to repair the tire. A cab would cost a fortune.

Normally they might have borrowed Sid and Marian's van, but her brother's family had gone to spend the week with Marian's parents in Sacramento.

Helene must have spent all day cooking just for the four of them. Karen had to get there.

She glared at the tire. She'd have to change it and put the spare through its paces.

She was in the process of digging everything out of the trunk, and realizing that after all these years the canister had probably gone dead, when Terry's bug *ooga-oogaed* up the street.

Funny how she'd managed to survive these past two years without a man, and now...

"Do you suppose we could borrow your car?" she asked as Terry popped out of the driver's seat. He'd just been to the local bookstore, judging from the logo on the paper sack he carried.

"Sure. Can you drive a stick shift?" he said. "You have to watch out for wind shear on the dragon's tail. It gets a little intense on the freeway. Where are you going? Need any help?"

And that was how, a few minutes and one telephone call to her mother later, Karen found herself and the kids loaded in with Terry, tootling along the freeway amid a flurry of weekend traffic.

Riding in a dragon was like nothing she'd ever experienced before.

People waved and honked. Children pressed their noses against window glass. Karen had never fully appreciated the diversity of Southern California's population until now, watching the rainbow of smiles that greeted the dragon's flight along the Pomona and Santa Monica freeways.

"Is it always like this?" she asked Terry.

"Like what?" He waved to a pair of children.

"I guess it must be." Outrageous vehicles clearly had more entertainment value than she'd suspected.

They reached West L.A. in just under an hour. Helene's condominium complex was tucked inside a nondescript neighborhood of apartment buildings, houses from the fifties, and strip shopping centers.

The condo itself offered a spacious cream expanse which, Karen noticed as they entered, had recently been enlivened with a brightly woven wall hanging from Mexico. She recalled that her mother had gone on a south-of-the-border junket with her garden-club friends in October. And already they were heading off to Santa Fe for the holidays. That must be quite some group of Golden Agers.

"Here you are!" Helene's new perm was set off by a handsome silver comb above one ear that gave her a rakish air. Her mother wore turquoise lounging pajamas that Karen had never seen before; usually Helene preferred shirtwaists.

"Grandma!" The children ran to offer the Christmas presents they'd made themselves—a crayoned drawing from Bopper, a misshapen scarf crocheted by Rose.

"These are wonderful!" Helene directed them into the den, where gaily wrapped packages awaited. "Your Mom doesn't mind if you open them now, does she?"

"Of course not." Karen had been counting on the diversion to allow her to explain about Terry. She hadn't had time to say much on the phone, except that a friend was giving them a ride.

She made the introduction, but before she could launch into any detail Terry said, "I am utterly charmed by you, Mrs. Joseph. I can see where Karen gets her beauty."

Helene smiled, clearly taken with his friendly teasing. "And you are everything Marian described."

Mentally, Karen chided her sister-in-law for gossiping. On the other hand, she knew Marian had probably been overcome by her natural enthusiasm.

"So glad to see my reputation precedes me," said Terry. "Can I help in the kitchen?"

"That's thoughtful of you." Helene glanced at her daughter. "Or perhaps the two of you would like to relax in the living room?"

Karen knew her mother wanted to encourage a potentially romantic relationship. But they hadn't come here to be alone and, besides, a relationship with Terry was the last thing she wanted.

"Terry's renting a room from me," Karen put in. "Until escrow closes."

Helene sighed. "In that case, Terry, would you like to ice the cake?"

"I thought you'd never ask." They sauntered off together like old friends.

Karen turned to close the door, then she saw an elderly man standing there. Perhaps elderly was the wrong word—although he must have been in his late sixties, there was nothing decrepit about him.

With a full head of salt-and-pepper hair, a firm, athletic build and an armful of Christmas presents, he looked like a Madison Avenue idealization of a grandfather. He also looked vaguely familiar.

"Karen?" said the man. "My goodness, you've grown!"

"You're..." She caught herself. "Frederick Baker!" He and his wife had occasionally joined her parents for a night out, years ago. But she'd heard nothing of him for ages. "Is your wife—?" She caught the glint of sadness. "Oh, I'm sorry."

"No need. She lived a full life." Frederick stepped inside. "Where are the children?"

The moment her mother came out to greet Frederick, things clicked into place for Karen. The way her mother slipped her arm through his, the little smiles they exchanged. This was the reason for the new hairstyle. And for taking so many trips.

She felt pleased for her mother, and yet a little lost, too. Helene had depended on her children, especially

Karen, for nearly fifteen years. Now Helene was breaking loose to establish her own life.

Perhaps, Karen told herself, she was making too much of this. All Helene had done was invite a man for dinner.

They ate a sumptuous meal of turkey and stuffing. Conversation flowed. If Helene and Frederick exchanged the occasional look of understanding, Karen chided herself for noticing. She was relieved that the children, oblivious to adult interaction, dug into their meal with relish.

Afterward they opened presents. Karen had brought her mother a selection of jams and teas, and was glad it could be shared with Frederick.

Her mother presented her with a hand-grown orchid plant. It would certainly brighten their new living room in the duplex.

For the children, Helene had selected clothes tailored to their tastes: a pink party dress for Rose and a sweatsuit for Bopper.

Then they all walked to a nearby park, where the children raced, cheering, toward the jungle gym. The December night was crisp but not cold, and Helene and Frederick made it clear they wanted the children to themselves.

Karen and Terry withdrew to a second play area across the park. He clambered onto a whirligig, a horseless merry-go-round. As Karen propped herself against the support bars, Terry lounged opposite her, spinning them slowly with one leg.

The streetlights muted to a blurry glow as they turned. The children's shouts faded to a murmur.

"This," Terry said, "is absolutely the only way to live. I could stay like this forever."

"It's not our whirligig," Karen reminded him.

"They're not our stars, either," he said. "Let go, Karen. Shake free. Float."

She closed her eyes. The gentle motion gave her a sense of being suspended in space. Past and future spun away, leaving only the uninterrupted moment.

Along the platform her knee came to rest against Terry's leg. It was a long leg, long and firm. Hardly thinking about what she was doing, she pressed her ankle along his lower leg. His knee was round and bony, and somehow her foot slipped to the inside, so her leg lay wound around his thigh.

A hand caught her ankle and massaged the sensitive tendons. The cool night air ruffled Karen's hair and prickled her neck and arms.

Terry's hand reached the inside of her knee. A rush of sensation caught Karen by surprise, flames dancing up her thighs and breasts. She sat up, catching her breath. Terry propped himself on one elbow as the whirligig slowed, and pulled her toward him.

Karen's lips parted instinctively. Centrifugal force turned everything to slow motion as his mouth closed over hers.

"Oops!" Terry sat up and stuck one foot onto the ground, slowing the carousel. Karen blinked, disoriented. Why had he stopped?

She heard the shouts only an instant before Bopper and Rose piled onto the whirligig. "Go, go!" Bopper cried.

"You're not getting *me* on that thing." Helene's chuckle drifted toward them.

"Me, either." Karen slid down, wobbled for a moment and caught hold of a swing set for support. The ground continued spinning for several seconds.

"Family life." Terry, still seated, kicked the ground to set the whirligig back into motion. "Can't beat it."

Karen thought she saw him wink at her as he and the kids spun into action.

THE REAL-ESTATE OFFICE was dead.

"Well, it *is* Christmas Eve," George grumbled as he paced through the outer office.

What would her boss do without his fourteen-hour-a-day job? Karen wondered. She sympathized with his wife and ten-year-old daughter, Bonnie, but they seemed to have gotten used to not having him around.

George harrumphed. "I suppose I could do a little farming." "Farming" was the real-estate term for knocking on doors in search of clients.

"People might not be in the mood to think about selling their houses today," Karen suggested.

His lips pinched together. Then he brightened. "You know, I haven't finished my own Christmas shopping. It would be nice to give Bonnie something that's just from me for a change, wouldn't it?"

"Good idea." Karen entertained the faintest of hopes that his next words might be, "And you can take the afternoon off."

Instead, he said, "Hold down the fort. Page me if you need me."

She came close to locking up the office and taking off anyway, but her conscience wouldn't let her. Wearily Karen settled down to checking through current escrows.

They were all in order—especially her own. All set to close right on time, the second of January.

IT WAS DARK WHEN Karen and the children turned onto their street. Bopper bounced in the back seat, keyed up about the holiday, while Rose sat in front clasping her doll.

She didn't say much about Bobby any more, but Karen knew the divorce in some ways had affected Rose most of all. Bopper talked about his father and openly missed him, but it was Rose who had nightmares, Rose who seemed prematurely adult since he'd left, Rose who fought to keep a tight grip on her little world—as if it might shatter at any moment.

"I love you," Karen told her daughter. "I love my little Rose and my little Bopper."

"We love you, too, Mommy," Rose said.

"What's that?" Bopper pointed ahead.

Karen braked to a halt. "That's our house," she said. "I think."

Her first impression was that someone had dropped part of Las Vegas into the middle of Whittier. She couldn't recall ever seeing so many flashing lights on one house before. Loops and whorls of red and green, blue and yellow, interlaced with purest white. Lights on the roof, in the trees, across the windowsills.

On the lawn, the glittering display of Santa's reindeer and elves would have done Disneyland proud.

"Oh, Mommy!" Rose cried. "It's beautiful!"

"Wow," said Bopper.

An adult voice inside Karen wanted to protest the garish excess, but she hushed it. The child in her loved the interplay of lights against the early winter darkness.

People were gathering on the sidewalk, neighbors and passersby, children and grown-ups. She could hear the appreciative murmur.

"Terry thinks of the best things," Rose said.

Karen put the car into gear and coasted forward, keeping a watchful eye out for pedestrians. They glided into the driveway as Terry bounded over.

"I hope you don't mind." He gestured toward another man Karen hadn't noticed before, a double for Sigmund Freud with his pointy beard and wire-rimmed eyeglasses.

"I'm Lou Loomis." The man shook hands with Karen as she extricated herself from the car. "Terry and I used to work together at the ad agency. I heard he'd bought a house and we had this stuff left over from a photo shoot, so I thought he might like it."

"That was thoughtful." Karen helped her children out. "Won't you join us for dinner?"

"We're sending out for pizza," Terry offered, to Karen's relief. She'd been trying to calculate which oddments in the refrigerator might be tossed together to make a dinner fit for company.

While they waited for the delivery man, Lou whipped out a recorder and a tambourine and performed "Jingle Bells." "My secret dream," he admitted afterward as he bowed to scattered applause, "is to become a one-man band. In the meantime, I masquerade as an art director."

The next few hours passed in a jumble of activity. More and more people gathered outside, occasionally bursting into Christmas carols. Terry was dissuaded from turning on the radio and blasting music out the door only when Karen and Lou pointed out that other neighbors might not appreciate it.

They might not appreciate the crowds and the lights either, Karen reflected, but that wasn't her problem. In another week, she thought sadly, they wouldn't be her neighbors anymore.

The whole evening took on bittersweet overtones. It was lovely to see Rose and Bopper devour their pizza and scamper back and forth to the front window to check the display. They loved it when Terry insisted on singing "Twas the Night before Christmas," more or less on key, as their bedtime story.

The events reminded Karen of how much she would miss this house. And Terry. Of course she could still see him, but...

But what? What could possibly happen between them? She had no time for a casual involvement, and Terry didn't strike her as the kind of man ready to take on a serious relationship. He was too mercurial and childlike. She loved those qualities, but she knew they would wear thin.

At nine o'clock Lou serenaded them with a ukulele rendition of "Rudolph the Red-nosed Reindeer," and headed off. With the children asleep, Karen had the pleasant task of arranging Christmas presents under the tree.

"You mean Santa isn't really coming?" Terry asked, when she offered him the milk and cookies the children had left by the hearth.

"He's already here." She smiled at him. "You've made this night special."

"No. It was special because...because you're here." Terry switched off the outside lights, leaving only a few strands of white to glimmer in the darkness.

"Or because it's Christmas Eve, and that's always special," she said.

Terry plucked a strand of popcorn from the tree and nibbled at it. "I want you to feel free to come back here, any time," he told her. "I'll put some toys and books in the children's rooms, and keep blueberry-muffin mix in the pantry."

He was being kinder than Karen wanted. "We have to start fresh," she said. "There are too many memories here. The children have to let go, and so do I."

"Are you saying you don't want to see me any more?" She'd never heard this note of quiet maturity in Terry's voice before. "I'm not one of your memories. I'm right here."

"It's just this feeling I have," she said. "That I've never completely let go of Bobby. I'm not ready to start something new, Terry."

He stared out at the night. Karen wanted to bring back the merriment that usually animated him, but anything she might have said would ring false.

"Good night," was the best she could do. "Merry Christmas."

"Merry Christmas." He remained at the window, shoulders squared like a sentinel, studying the row of old-fashioned houses across the street with their modest trims of colored lights.

When she finished checking the door locks and went upstairs, he was still standing there.

TERRY HADN'T WISHED on a star since childhood. He wasn't consciously wishing on one now, but his jumbled thoughts formed a request: let her decide to stay.

He knew Karen couldn't be teased or argued into staying. Some force greater than either of them, or some unforeseen stroke of chance, would have to change her mind.

The best he could do was to help make tomorrow special, for all of them.

Chapter Five

On Christmas morning, Rose woke up before anyone else. She could tell no one was stirring, because the floor would have creaked and the heating vents would have carried any noises from downstairs.

She lay with her arms around her doll, feeling her flannel gown bunched under her hips. She tried to remember what she'd dreamed last night, but it was gone. Mommy said you always dreamed, even if you didn't remember it. It must have been about Christmas; now she caught it, a faint image of furry mice wearing plaid bows around their necks, holding little choir books and singing by the tree.

Rose sat up, put on her embroidered velvet slippers and tiptoed into the hall. Her mother's door was ajar; she could hear Mommy's regular breathing. From the guest room came Terry's deeper rumble, not a snore really, but a kind of echo—as if his lungs were so big the air rattled around for a while before it came out.

It felt quite powerful, to be the only one awake in the whole house. Rose checked the hall clock and saw that it was almost six o'clock. Maybe they'd sleep for a whole hour longer.

She walked downstairs. In the early morning darkness, something sparkled off to her right. She glanced quickly, but it was only dust motes in the first rays of dawn light. Or maybe fairy dust.

Her heart thudded into her throat as she caught sight of the tree and the presents. That bright paper! That gleaming ribbon and the fancy bows, and the little silver bells! And the tiny teddy bears peeping out of the two stockings on the mantel! Rose could hardly keep from grabbing everything.

She walked to the tree and sorted out the gifts that were marked with her name. This year she could read the cards, not just look at the drawings of reindeer and angels. There was one from Grandma Helene, and one from Uncle Sid and Aunt Marian, and of course several from Mommy. She didn't suppose she should open anything until Mommy came down, though.

It meant something, to be the first one up on Christmas morning. She could feel excitement welling up from some point outside herself. Something was going to happen. Something so special and wonderful it could only occur on Christmas. Something like...

Tears tickled at her eyes. She hadn't meant to think about Daddy coming back home. She knew stuff like that didn't really happen except on TV, and not even very often then. Stories seemed to have these happy-sad endings, like Pollyanna falling out of a tree or Old Yeller getting shot. On Christmas she wanted a happy-happy ending, and she wanted it now.

Rose heard a noise. Not a footstep or a cough but a funny little rustling, off in the kitchen.

She put the presents down and glided across the room. There it was again! And a little thump.

Rose reached the kitchen door and looked around. There weren't any Borrowers poised for flight on the floor, or a Charlotte-the-Spider spinning words into a web up by the ceiling. But she knew that rustling had meant something special, because she'd wished for it so hard.

There! The laundry room!

Rose burst into a run, skidding to a stop just past the doorway.

A watchful pair of chinchilla eyes met hers. Gloompuss! Then Phil poked his nose over his wife's shoulder. She could swear he was smiling.

Something else stuck out of the pile of cedar shavings. Two small furry tails.

Rose stepped forward. She could see them clearly now, two baby chinchillas as cute and bright-eyed as their parents. "Oh! Look!" she gasped, and the babies popped out of the shavings to peer at her.

They weren't at all like the baby hamsters she'd seen once at a classmate's house, naked and blind and squirming. These little guys were fully furred and ready to play.

"Can I hold you?" Rose slipped open the cage door and reached inside. She started to pull back when Gloompuss chattered angrily, but one of the babies hopped right into her hand.

Rose lifted it to her cheek. "You were born on Christmas Day. I'll call you Noel. And the other one could be Tinsel."

After a minute, Rose put the baby back. Then she sat for a long time, watching the chinchillas groom themselves and cuddle.

It was a miracle, that yesterday there had been two of the soft creatures and now there were four. A miracle that had happened especially for Rose.

Wishes did come true. Sometimes they really did.

THE LETDOWN SET IN shortly after lunch.

Karen had awakened about seven, to find Rose already in the kitchen setting out the pancake mix. The morning flew by in a blur of breakfast, presents, baby chinchillas, attending church and coming home for lunch to find that Terry had left without a word.

Karen didn't see why that should bother her. He wasn't a member of the family. She'd made that clear to him last night, hadn't she?

The overcast sky weighed on her spirits, and so did the absence of her brother, sister-in-law and mother. She felt isolated, carrying the weight of the children's expectations entirely on herself.

She hadn't missed the way Bopper kept glancing at the telephone. Waiting for the call from Daddy that never came.

In the afternoon, after settling the children in their rooms for quiet time, Karen came downstairs to face torn wrapping paper, a nativity jigsaw puzzle with pieces scattered on, under and around the couch, and a kitchen full of dirty lunch dishes.

Where were the elves when she needed them?

An hour later, Karen settled onto the couch in the den. From a rack of magazines, she pulled out a very special catalog.

It wasn't a wish book from a department store or a mail-order house. It was an offering for the future. A future that Karen didn't have time for yet. But maybe, as soon as she could save a little money...

She flipped hungrily through the course catalog from the local community college, skipping to the business section.

Karen had taken enough basic classes before her marriage to earn an associate of arts degree. She knew it might be years, maybe never, before she'd find time to go on for a bachelor's. But if she could squeeze in the right classes, she could qualify for a better job.

She flipped happily through the pages. She couldn't imagine most people thrilling to Principles of Retailing or Human Relations in Business, but the course descriptions sent possibilities shimmering through her mind.

She loved organizing things and working with people. She'd like to move into management, with a small company at first and then perhaps a bigger one.

Karen daydreamed through the catalog. It was a rare indulgence, but once they were settled in their new home and she began saving money, why not take a class? Maybe next summer...

"Mommy?" Bopper stood in the doorway. "Could we put the jigsaw puzzle together?"

Karen glanced at her watch. The children had been upstairs for almost two hours. "Sure!"

The three of them gathered around the dining-room table and began fitting pieces into place. It grew dark outside. Karen hadn't planned anything special for Christmas supper, just a pasta dish the children liked. She knew she ought to feel contented, but an undercurrent of restlessness told her something was missing.

Where had Terry gone?

Another week and he'd be out of their lives, anyway. Busy, no doubt, with his fellow writers and—what *did* a horror novelist do when he wasn't writing?

Speaking engagements, book signings, research? How did you research vampires, anyway? Karen wasn't sure she'd care to find out.

"Mommy," Rose said. "I hear sleigh bells."

"That's the wind chimes next door." Karen seized a lamb for the nativity scene and slotted it into place. "Got it!"

"I hear them, too," said Bopper.

Karen stopped searching for a calf. That did sound like sleigh bells, right in front of the house.

She heard footsteps and then a sharp yip-yip.

Bopper didn't say the word "Daddy," but his little mouth framed it. Rose shook her head. "He wouldn't go to that much trouble," she said. "He'd expect *us* to entertain *him*."

When had a seven-year-old gotten so wise?

"Ho-ho-ho!" shouted Terry from the front porch.

"What do reindeer say?" came a female voice.

"Come in!" Karen was heading for the door when it burst open. In spilled Terry, much too tall for his Santa Claus suit, Joni Rodd, wearing a brown cap with reindeer horns, and two boisterous puppies squirming in Joni's arms.

"Terry got his chinches and I got my pups!" she declared. "I named them Donner and Blitzen."

"Can I hold one?" the children chorused, as if they'd rehearsed it. Joni deposited one puppy in each pair of eager arms.

From over his shoulder, Terry unslung a large beach bag. "Southern California special delivery!" he announced, and hauled out an assortment of odd-shaped packages. "Ho-ho-ho!" Then he gazed around suspiciously. "Where's the cookies?"

"I didn't bake any," Karen confessed.

He shook his head. "Wrong house." And started to collect the presents.

"No!" Rose leaped to stop him. Her puppy wriggled away.

"Look out—" Karen noticed Bopper wasn't holding his little dog any more, either.

"I'll clean up after them," Joni promised. "Really, I don't mind."

"It's just—" Karen glanced helplessly at the Christmas tree, strung with cookies and candy canes and popcorn balls. "Don't you think they might—"

Might, and could, and were already on their way to wreak havoc, she realized even as she spoke.

Later, she wished she had had a video camera to record the scene, because it must have looked hilarious. Three grown-ups, two of them prancing around in ridiculous costumes, trying to catch two puppies who were leaping and chomping and spinning pine needles everywhere. Popcorn flew under the couch, cookies disintegrated, and the whole time Bopper was tearing open present after present, even the ones that weren't for him.

"Gotcha!" Joni hauled one pup from behind the tree as Karen nabbed the other by the collar. "You little troublemakers! I knew I shouldn't have brought them, but I couldn't bear to leave them home. Not on Christmas."

"Santa will vacuum," Terry reassured her.

"It's fine," Karen told Joni, adding with a sidelong look at Terry, "And, yes, Santa will vacuum."

She took in the scene, the children happily digging through their gifts, Terry dancing about red-cheeked, and Joni getting her face washed by two little pink tongues.

Confusion and noise. Just what this house needed to get into the holiday spirit.

Bopper received a windup train; Karen was glad Terry hadn't spent hundreds of dollars on an electric set. With the radio-controlled car she'd given him, Bopper was in heaven.

A book of punch-out Victorian dolls and doll clothes was hugged to Rose's chest. She couldn't choose between preserving the book as it was, and removing the dolls to play with.

The best present turned out to be still hiding in the Volkswagen: two roasted chickens and an assortment of salads from a deli Terry had found open. Everyone crowded around the dining-room table, eating and chattering while the puppies went to sleep in the kitchen.

"This is the best Christmas ever," Bopper announced when Terry pulled out a sack of chocolate éclairs for dessert.

"Is it?" Karen asked Rose. Her daughter seemed happy today, but Rose tended to keep her deepest thoughts to herself.

"It's best enough," the little girl said, and snatched one of the éclairs before Bopper could corner the market.

Karen caught Terry's eye across the table. "Thank you."

"It's the bestest Christmas I ever had, either," he said.

Joni seized the opportunity to read bedtime stories to Rose and Bopper. She acted them out with all the enthusiasm of a born teacher, and soon the children slid into bed with eyelids drooping.

Joni and the puppies exited next, taking along an assortment of torn wrapping paper and bows as playthings. Scarcely was she out the door, when Terry, as good as his word, shucked his Santa Claus costume and vacuumed the living room.

"This was wonderful," Karen said as he clicked off the noise. "You have just the right touch with the children."

"Isn't that why kids were put here, so we can all relive our childhoods and make them come out right?" Terry stored the machine and plunged out the back door. He returned with an armful of logs for the fireplace.

"It's been a long time," Karen admitted as they sat on the living-room rug watching the flames crackle. "I never get around to building one."

Wavering light danced across Terry's face. His eyes took on a faraway look as he gazed into the fire, and his mouth quirked with unaccustomed sadness.

"What did you mean, make our childhoods come out right?" Karen prodded gently. "Was there something wrong with yours?"

"Have you ever been to Amherst?" Terry asked. "Massachusetts?"

She shook her head.

"It's a college town," he said. "Beautiful place, especially in the fall. Ruled by trees. With little shops. Quaint enough for Emily Dickinson to come home to, even now."

Karen stretched back on the rug, resting her head on a cushion. She'd never traveled farther east than Arizona, but she summoned up an image from old movies, and found herself moved by an unfamiliar nostalgia.

"My grandmother lived there all her life," Terry said. "She had only one son, my father, and she was forty when he was born—ancient, in those days. He was always into mischief, people tell me."

"What about your grandfather?"

"He died when Dad was ten," Terry said. "Anyway, to get to the point of all this, Dad literally ran away to join the circus when he was fifteen."

"Your poor grandmother." Karen closed her eyes, floating in the warmth from the hearth. "I didn't know you could really do that."

"He lied about his age. Anyway, he had talent. As a clown. That's where he met my mother—she came from a family of acrobats." Terry chuckled. "Can you believe this? I didn't even make it up."

"It does account for certain aspects of your personality," Karen teased.

When he didn't reply, she turned to look, and saw that his eyes glittered a deeper blue than usual, the blue of unshed tears. "My mother died in an accident when I was five," he said. "I was sent to live at Grandma's house."

"Where the trees ruled," she murmured.

He shot her a glance full of appreciation. "Grandma must have been near seventy. After all the heartache from my father, I guess she didn't want to get too involved with me. What I remember most is the silence. It echoed in that old house."

Karen could feel the rest: the coldly proper holidays, the lonely evenings in his room, the old-fashioned clothes that isolated him from his classmates. Until at some point Terry learned to play the clown, too.

"What happened to your father?" she asked.

"Unfortunately, he developed a problem with alcohol." Terry released a deep breath. "He married again, a couple of times, actually. He lives in Boston with a group of over-the-hill entertainers. They left their hearts with the street theater of the sixties and seventies. We don't have much to say to each other, but I send him money from time to time."

"You never got close," she said.

"There was no point." He leaned forward and stirred the fire. "Not everything can have a storybook ending."

It was a lot to think about—Terry's strange childhood, his remote clown of a father. And the words, "There was no point." No point in getting close to his father.

That was what she sensed, under Terry's warmth and good-heartedness. That he kept his deepest feelings in check.

But, then, didn't she?

KAREN WASN'T AWARE she'd fallen asleep until the telephone woke her. She heard Terry's voice speaking softly in the kitchen, and then he came into the living room.

"I'm sorry to wake you," he said. "It's for you."

Sleepily, Karen wondered who would call so late. She was starting to worry that something had happened to her mother or brother, when she heard the nasal voice of her soon-to-be landlord, Harvey Weir.

"Mrs. Loesser? I'm sorry to disturb you on Christmas, but something's come up," he said.

"Come up?" She found herself thinking, *Well, if we have to delay moving for a week or two, that wouldn't be so bad. Let that be all, please, please.*

But it wasn't. "Fact is, my daughter just called from Santa Fe. She and her husband are splitting up. She's coming out here with the kids and, well, she needs a place to stay. So I promised her the duplex."

"Mr. Weir." Karen took a deep breath. "I signed a rental agreement."

"Month to month," he reminded her. "I'm sure you don't want to move in there for thirty days and then have to leave. I know this is inconvenient and I feel just awful, but I don't see what else I can do. I called you today so you could start right away tomorrow to line up something else."

Karen was so angry she didn't dare speak. So she did the only thing she could think of—she slammed down the phone.

"Damn him!" she yelled to the refrigerator, which made a vague grumbling noise as if in agreement. "Why can't *she* find a place to live? Why do I have to take the consequences of other people's problems?"

It wasn't necessarily impossible to rent a place in a week. She supposed she could find an apartment in one of those giant complexes, but it would be farther from Sid and Marian's house. And it wouldn't have a yard.

Even as she tried to tell herself that this was hardly a life-threatening emergency, Karen leaned against the table and burst into tears.

There was the quiet creak of floorboards, and then two large hands cradled hers. "Went back on his word?"

"His daughter's moving in." Karen bit her lip to stem the tears. She didn't like anyone to see her this vulnerable. Not her, the girl who'd taken control and kept it since she was sixteen.

"You could always stay here," Terry said.

"Thanks. Really. But I want us to get settled." Karen removed one hand from his grasp and wiped her eyes. In an emergency, there was nothing like your sleeve. "This is hard enough on the kids as it is."

"I didn't mean just while you were looking." He leaned so close she could feel his breath warming her cheek. "Think about it. What am I going to do with this whole house to myself? I'll probably end up renting out a couple of rooms anyway."

"No," Karen said.

He pushed on. "I'll charge whatever you were going to pay for the duplex. That's fair, isn't it? Full kitchen privileges. Think about it. You'll save on moving expenses. The kids can keep their rooms. We've lived this way for a week already with no problems."

"Gee, a whole week." She couldn't help teasing. "That long?"

"And I like the company." Terry brushed his lips across her forehead. "Think about me rattling around here by myself. And the poor baby chinchillas, nobody to play with. And your ex-husband will probably come bursting in here the middle of some night and find all this empty space and invite his whole art colony to move in."

Karen couldn't stifle a smile. She wouldn't put it past Bobby, that was for sure.

"Look," she said before she weakened, "I'll find something. Really, in the long run, it's for the best."

"Take Dr. Vogel's advice." He ruffled the back of her hair. "Stay where you belong."

"I...can't." She couldn't meet his eyes. After a while, the floor boards creaked away.

Karen stood in the kitchen inhaling the leftover odors of chicken and pine, chocolate and cedar.

The thing she valued most about this house wasn't the memories—it was how solidly these walls had been built and how carefully the floors had been laid, nearly a century ago.

She'd spent enough time in apartments to know that they felt different. That the walls were thin, the windows never leveled quite right, the floors installed sloppily. Cracker-box construction by people who didn't care. That's what she minded most, right now.

When noises overhead reassured her that Terry really had retreated, Karen let herself wander through the dining room and into the front.

The dying flames played shadows over the curtains she'd stitched herself and the molding she'd lovingly restored. At the far end of the room, light glimmered off a small stained-glass window she'd bought in a secondhand shop.

She had to give in, at least for now. This was her home, hers and Rose's and Bopper's.

But only for a little while, Karen told herself firmly. No longer than she had to.

Chapter Six

What exactly *was* hiding in Old Lady Maycap's closet?

Terry leaned back in his desk chair and closed his eyes so he wouldn't see the cursor blinking on the computer screen like a silent nag. Not so silent, when you considered that faint but insistent electrical hum.

He missed his old manual typewriter.

From outside, down below, came the chutter-chutter of a jalopy rumbling down the street. Further off, from Whittier Boulevard, he heard the wheeze of a bus. The workaday world.

That was what made writing horror so much fun. Finding dark shadows in the bland sunshine. Inventing little frights, scaring people until they laughed. People loved a good shock, as long as they could wake up from it safe and sound.

Before he'd found salvation as the class clown, Terry had buried himself in books. The further they carried him from reality, the better. *Dr. Dolittle, David and the Phoenix, One Hundred and One Dalmatians*. Now he created the same kind of escapism for grown-ups.

As long as he was sitting here letting his mind wander, he let it linger on the memory of how Karen had looked this morning. She'd worn a new pink blouse that enlivened her gray eyes and made her skin glow. Maybe he could talk her into growing her hair a little longer. He suspected the light brown would yield some russet highlights, given the chance.

On the other hand, he'd better not press her too hard to loosen up. She'd agreed to stay until Rose finished school for the summer, and that was more than he'd dared hope.

There was a sense of stability about Karen that he cherished, along with a nurturing quality that helped soothe those long untended needs left over from childhood. Yet what Terry liked best were the rare flashes of vulnerability, the times when she needed him.

Well, thinking about all that wouldn't solve his problem. With his usual enthusiasm, he'd launched a quarter of the way into *Dream a Little Scream of Me* without actually figuring out what it was about. Exactly what *was* it that old Gladys Maycap had just retrieved from the back of her candy store and transferred to the hall closet of her moldering manor? What was this beast that insinuated itself year by year into her soul, until there was only a trifle of Gladys left?

Terry propped his feet on either side of the word processor. He'd encountered the same problem with his last book, *The Ghoul of the Golden West,* and it had worked out splendidly. Things always did.

It was hard not to fantasize about what might happen when *Ghoul* finally came out. With the promotion his editor was promising, it might move his name up from the steady-but-unexciting ranks of journeyman horror writers onto the bestseller lists.

Then there was the promised film version of *Major League Vampire.* When it was released, it would spur sales of the paperback edition. He wouldn't mind that at all, hitting hard- and softcover lists at the same time. But for now...

The thing in the closet. A miasma. Terry liked the sound of the word. He hauled out his *Synonym Finder* and looked it up. Good heavens. Fetor, reek, stench. No, the thing couldn't smell that bad and still sneak up on people.

He wanted it to be something ancient, but not a vengeful Indian spirit; that was becoming a cliché. Which meant it had to have been brought to Buffalo, New York from the Middle East or Asia, perhaps hidden inside a mummy or a vase. Or a religious relic.

Now, there was a possibility. What if some Arab merchant in the Middle Ages had mistaken an ancient evil being for a manifestation of divinity and carried it back to North Africa? Centuries later, a priest—make that a missionary—was seduced by the spirit inside the carved stone bottle and brought it all the way to Buffalo? In the dark of the long winters on the shores of Lake Erie, the thing had festered...

Terry plopped his feet down and began to write.

KAREN SAW THE KITE all the way from Whittier Boulevard, before she turned. A Japanese demon kite, swooping and swirling in the January breeze.

Her thought began with, I wonder who...and trailed off into the usual, Who else?

She wondered when Terry found a chance to work. He always seemed to be on the move when she was home, but perhaps that was the natural reaction to becoming a home owner. He found innumerable ways to improve the place, from nailing down roof shingles to giving the exterior a much-needed coat of paint.

It was hard, Karen reflected as she pulled into the driveway, to remember that the house didn't belong to her any more. She had to bite her tongue to stop from commenting when Terry decided to repaint the kitchen in glowing peach—which actually did look rather nice, now that he was finished. Or she would catch herself thinking that someday she'd like to add on a downstairs bedroom and then remember that it wasn't her decision to make.

She was just renting. But it didn't feel like it.

Karen parked in the driveway, dropped off some groceries in the kitchen and went out back to watch the kite.

"That's it! That's it! Reel it in just a little—fight the wind—there! Look at it go! Terry perched atop the low stone wall that separated their yard from the neighbor's, calling directions to Rose.

"Mommy!" Bopper hopped up and down. "Look at us! Look at the dragon!"

"It's beautiful." She folded her arms. "Terry, I hate to criticize, but what are the kids doing home?"

"I picked them up at Marian's—watch out! Back up, back up! Going to crash— No, no— Thank goodness for stray breezes!" Terry, who accompanied his commands with appropriate body English, sank back onto the wall.

"It's lucky I decided to drop the food off first and then go get the kids," Karen murmured.

Guilt flashed across his face. "I'm sorry. I didn't think. I was so excited about the kite, I couldn't wait to pick them up. I should have called— No, Rose! Let it go! Let it go!"

The kite string had snagged a tree. Rose gave up jerking it as a gust of wind yanked the whole construction into the sky in a series of fits and starts.

"Oh, Terry! I'm sorry," Rose wailed.

"You lost it!" Bopper raged at his sister.

"Whoa." Terry grabbed Bopper's arm with his free hand. "Couldn't you tell? The dragon had to go chase a fire demon in the sky."

"I didn't see no demon," Bopper muttered.

"Any demon," corrected Rose.

"Of course not." Terry led them all toward the house. "Fire demons live on the other side of the sun and human people can't see them."

"And don't you ever look at the sun," Karen reminded her children. "It'll burn your eyes."

Turning, she nearly tripped over a curved sheet of wire mesh. "Good heavens. I'm afraid to ask."

"Thought I'd build a chinchilla run this weekend." Terry negotiated the steps to the porch and held the back door for her. "The little ones need fresh air."

"Isn't it kind of cold?" Karen set her sack down on the kitchen table and answered her own question, "But I guess not, since they're from the Andes."

"What's for dinner?" Setting his load beside hers, Terry deftly emptied it. "Pepperoni! Dare I hope! And fresh tomatoes! Zucchini . . . ! Zucchini pizza?"

"Rigatoni!" cried Bopper. "My favorite! Only don't give me any of the zucchini, Mommy, okay?"

"My own variation on a recipe by the Frugal Gourmet." Karen tucked odds and ends into the refrigerator. "Rigatoni with pepperoni and tomatoes. I started adding zucchini from my garden last summer, when it was coming out our ears, and I like it."

Without being asked, Rose removed a large pot from the cabinet, filled it with water and put it on the stove. She anticipated Karen's needs in a way that was a little eerie.

There was nothing peculiar with a seven-year-old acting helpful, Karen reminded herself. In a lot of ways, Rose reminded her of herself. What was wrong with being a little overresponsible, in an age when half the people you met shirked responsibility for everything?

"Mommy," Rose said, "the stove won't light."

"I'll do it." Karen flicked on the burner, but there was no familiar hiss of escaping gas. She checked the pilot lights and saw they were both off.

"This old thing," she grumbled. "Sometimes it turns itself off—some kind of outdated safety mechanism. You have to practically take the thing apart to get it started again."

The weight of a long day groaned onto her shoulders. Bopper had awakened her at six. Then she'd arrived to find George having one of his busy days—clients dropping by unannounced, an escrow threatening to blow up two days before the closing—and she hadn't even eaten lunch.

"I'll do it," Terry said.

Karen stared at the pile of food. The rigatoni dish was relatively easy to fix, but she felt too tired to slice a single tomato.

"Maybe we could have this tomorrow," she said. "I'll send out... But we had pizza two days ago, didn't we?"

"That's okay," Bopper assured her.

"I'll make a salad." Rose retrieved lettuce from the refrigerator.

"Whoa." Terry steered Karen to a chair. "You've been cooking ever since I moved in here."

"But you do the dishes," she pointed out.

"Nevertheless." He prowled into the pantry. "I knew I saw some corn chips in here. And *frijoles*. Rose, you chop up those tomatoes and shred some lettuce. I'll grate cheese. We're having taco salad!"

Despite some dubious comments from Bopper, Rose and Terry pitched in and soon had their makeshift meal on the table. With the Mexican beans heated in the microwave, it tasted wonderful, although they had to make do with plain yogurt instead of sour cream as a topping.

"It's better with guacamole," Terry sighed as they finished off the chips. "Maybe I could plant an avocado tree. How long do they take to bear fruit?"

"Years," Karen said.

"We could do that." Terry grinned. "That's the point of being a home owner, isn't it?"

Karen glanced around the table, and that was when she noticed the best thing of all. So many times over the past two years, despite her efforts, their dinner companion had been a ghostly Bobby, stifling every effort at conversation, reminding them how once upon a time he'd amused and diverted them.

The memory figure was gone. Terry had displaced him, a real live friend who brought giggles to Rose's throat and chased the unnatural dark cloud from Bopper's spirits.

We don't argue so much, she realized. *We don't sit here silently blaming each other, and ourselves, and Bobby. It's as if he's finally, really gone. Well, almost.*

"Anyone for bingo?" Terry asked.

"Me! Me!" cried Bopper, who couldn't actually follow the numbers but loved to have Karen help with his card.

"I'll call!" Rose cleared away the dishes, and for once her brother rushed to help.

They played three rounds, and then Karen bathed the children while Terry finished cleaning up.

When each child was tucked in and kissed two or three times, Karen slipped out into the hall with Terry. This was the ticklish part, she'd discovered these past two weeks. What to do in the evening with a man who was less than a lover and more than a casual friend.

Sometimes he left for his writer's group, or to attend a lecture or movie. Sometimes Karen was so exhausted she retreated to her room, read for a little while and fell asleep.

But tonight was Friday. She felt recovered from her earlier weariness and filled with a restless, almost adolescent ache to have fun.

"Let's go dancing," Terry murmured close to her ear. His breath tickled.

"But..."

"Slip on something charming. Meet you downstairs." He vanished into his room.

How did Terry manage to fill the air with this champagne effervescence? Karen floated giddily off. Surely she couldn't be responding this way to such a simple thing as feeling his baritone rumble across her nerve endings. He must have drugged the food.

Charming, he'd said. There was a word that didn't apply to Karen's wardrobe, she mused as she surveyed the contents.

She owned several tailored dresses and suits appropriate for work, along with the Southern California

mother's uniform of jeans and T-shirts. As for little
frilly nothings, they'd played no role in her life for
many years.

Bobby's idea of a night out had been to attend a
gallery opening at which the guests were divided into
rich patrons wearing designer originals, and the artists
and their spouses, clad in torn jeans.

Karen prowled through the walk-in closet, inspecting the contents. Then she noticed a glint of blue in the
very back. It didn't stir even the faintest hint of a
memory.

Karen lifted the garment into the clear light of the
bedroom. Where had it come from?

With its scooped neck and puffed three-quarter
sleeves, the dress sang of romantic evenings *à deux*. It
swirled below the knees, the satiny blue fabric woven
with silver butterflies.

She felt as if a fairy godmother had delivered the
dress with one wave of the wand.

*It's much too young for me. I don't know why I
bought it.*

There! She *did* remember! Her mother had presented her with the dress not long after Bobby left. At
the time, Karen had scarcely glanced at it, not feeling
in any mood to go partying. Now, examining the
beautiful workmanship, she realized that the gown
hadn't really been a hand-me-down at all—that Helene
must have purchased it in the hopes of cheering Karen
up.

She sat on the bed, the dress folded over one arm,
thanking her mother for the thoughtfulness she hadn't
recognized at the time.

Her heart skipping, Karen slipped into the dress and added a delicate silver necklace and earrings. Only then did she dare inspect herself in the mirror.

The lamplight highlighted an image she hadn't seen in years, a young, high-spirited Karen ready for a night out. The blue lent her eyes a deep smoky luster, while the silver ornaments brought out a trace of pink in her cheeks.

Or was it the thought of Terry that made her blush?

They couldn't really be going out, of course, Karen reminded herself, not without a baby-sitter. Was she making too much of his invitation? Well, so what if she was? Terry had said to dress up.

Slipping on a pair of silver sandals, Karen glided down the stairs.

A teasing scent met her halfway. Nothing as obvious as incense, but a faint exotic aroma that she couldn't quite place. The soft lilt of a Loggins and Messina album drifted to her ears.

From the hall, Terry stepped forward wearing a black-and-white tuxedo, complete right down to the pleated cummerbund and neat bow tie.

"You . . . *own* a tuxedo?" she said.

Terry quirked an eyebrow and brought her hand to his lips.

"And what—" she couldn't seem to stop chattering "—what *is* that wonderful aroma?"

"Earl Grey tea." He dropped one arm around her waist and caught her hand in his. "May I have this dance?"

"I'm sorry, but I'm sure I promised it to the duke," Karen said.

''The duke has been detained.'' His cheek pressed against her hair as he whirled her into the misty dining room.

Had the tea steam gotten into the air? Karen spotted a gauzy scarf draped over the chandelier, softening the light. A child's trick, but it worked. In the hazy atmosphere, Karen felt drawn into another dimension, transformed into a fairy-tale princess claiming her dance with the prince.

The music slowed. Terry's arm tightened around her waist and Karen moved with his rhythm. She felt tuned to the slightest tension in his arms and thigh muscles.

It was dangerous to think too much about those muscles, but the music blocked everything else from Karen's thoughts. His skin radiated heat along her body. His legs grazed hers in a dance as old as time. His shoulders protected her from the world.

She let Terry guide her. A heavy cloak of responsibility dissipated into the air. Karen rippled with long-hidden hungers.

Terry's mouth teased her temple. It was a subtle gesture, but sensations flooded through her arteries. She could feel every shift of the air currents, taste every flavor in the air.

With a deep sigh, Karen leaned into him, letting the space between them evaporate. This was no longer dancing but lovemaking, a deeply arousing, slowly building fire.

His thumb rubbed along her jaw, tipping up her chin. She thought he was going to kiss her, but his lips found her cheek first, her nose, the corner of an eye. Karen stood on the balls of her feet. They touched knee to knee, hip to hip.

With infinite slowness, Terry's mouth came down on hers, tasting, exploring. His hand caught the back of her head and held her.

As his tongue mastered the depths of her mouth, his hands stroked along her back. Karen had no will to resist as his fingers circled forward along her sides until they teased the edges of her breasts. Despite his gentleness, she felt herself hypnotized.

She ached for more, for an edge of roughness, and then he caught her against him, one palm pressing her breast until it flowered with longing. He lowered her onto the couch and ran his hands along her as if laying claim.

Then she heard the noise. Unwillingly, cursing her own acute awareness. Car doors slamming in the driveway. Two voices, one masculine and one feminine. Footsteps on the walkway.

"Oh, damn!" Karen said.

The doorbell rang. "Ignore it," he whispered.

"Karen?" It was Marian. She would have heard the music—no pretending the house was empty. In fact, if she didn't answer the door, she knew her brother and sister-in-law would probably let themselves in with their spare key, and wouldn't that be embarrassing!

Terry shrugged, heaved a sigh and stood up. Karen straightened her dress and wondered how much her jumbled emotions showed on her face.

"Oh, dear," Marian said when she opened the door. "We've interrupted something."

"We left Lisa with a baby-sitter and had dinner out," Sid explained, his honest, square face alight with amusement. "Just thought we'd drop by for some adult conversation."

"*Monsieur et madame,* your table is ready." Karen turned to see Terry, a white napkin draped over his arm, waiter style, bowing to their guests.

"We really should be going," Marian quavered.

Sid stepped inside. "Oh, come on. We've already embarrassed the hell out of my sister. Why stop now?"

Karen couldn't help but laugh. He was right—he might as well come in. All her inhibitions had snapped back into place the moment she saw them, and she'd never be able to get back in the mood now.

"Your table, *monsieur,*" Terry repeated.

He ushered them into the kitchen, where she discovered that he'd draped the table with a white lace cloth and set out a bottle of wine, a teapot and an assortment of ceramic mugs.

"Teacups?" Sid asked. "For wine?"

"Couldn't find the glasses," Terry admitted.

"Oh." Karen shook her head. "I forgot—I packed them. I don't drink wine very often..."

"See if I leave a tip," said her brother, and sat down.

"We do have Earl Grey, also," Terry advised.

They sipped their drinks, Sid enjoying the situation, Terry making light of it, and Marian and Karen exchanging sympathetic glances.

Why didn't things ever happen this way in the movies? She couldn't imagine Richard Gere and Julia Roberts being interrupted while lost in passion.

Was that what she'd been? Lost in passion?

The realization of what had nearly happened struck Karen for the first time. What on earth had she been thinking? Yes, Terry was wonderfully romantic, fun to be with and good for the kids. But nothing he'd done had changed her initial impression that he wasn't the sort of man to count on in a pinch. Not if it threatened his devil-may-care existence.

Already she was living in his house; already the children were growing attached. She had to keep an essential distance before they all got hurt.

"Maybe we could dance," Marian said at last. "Before I get too tipsy to stand up."

"She's a lightweight." Sid patted his wife's shoulder fondly. "All we had was a beer with dinner."

"Sounds like a fancy dinner," Karen teased.

"What else would you drink with shrimp?" Her brother feigned indignation.

The music on the tape changed. Karen recognized the charged rhythms of Creedence Clearwater Revival. Her body began to sway.

"This sure brings back memories." Sid stood up. "Let's dance."

"I thought you'd never ask," Marian teased.

Karen and Terry joined in, letting the music fill them with energy. By the time her brother and sister-in-law left, Karen felt relaxed, glowing with exertion—and not at all romantic.

"YOU DON'T THINK..." Marian let the words trail away.

"Think what?" Sid demanded as he steered around a bicycle some child had left in the street. "That my sister was on the brink of compromising herself? She's a grown woman. She can do what she likes."

"Well, she wouldn't really have..." Now, why was she worrying about that? "Okay, okay, it's none of my business."

"Why shouldn't she?" Sid demanded with hardheaded doggedness. "She's a good-looking woman. He seems like a nice guy. Think I'd let some jerk live with my sister?"

"Oh? And exactly how would you stop him?" Marian refrained from pointing out that Bobby had turned out to be "some jerk." She knew Sid blamed himself because he'd introduced them; Bobby had been the accountant at Sid's trucking firm.

Sid considered the question as he pulled into their driveway. "I'd hang around," he said. "Get my buddies to do the same. Stay under his feet, keep an eye on him. Make him so nervous he'd move out."

"It's his house." She gathered up her purse.

"Then he'd find a place for her to move to." Sid opened his door and headed for the front porch. He hadn't held a door for Marian since their courtship days, but she didn't mind. Her husband might lack social graces, but he was a good man.

She paid the baby-sitter and went to check on Lisa while Sid drove the teenager home.

On her way down the hall, Marian noticed toys scattered around the spare bedroom and went in to straighten up. It doubled as a playroom, which helped keep Lisa from messing up the den.

Marian retrieved a couple of dolls and assorted tiny doll clothes and went to dump them in the crib. That was when it hit her, the twist of longing that she usually pushed to the back of her mind.

When Lisa outgrew the crib a year ago, Marian had moved it in here expecting to have another baby to tuck into it before long. But it hadn't worked out that way.

They'd been trying for two years now. That wasn't really so long—it had taken her a year and a half to get pregnant with Lisa. But now that she'd had a child, Marian had expected it to be easy the second time.

They couldn't afford infertility treatments. Her regular doctor had checked her and Sid; he'd prescribed some vitamins and suggested using an ovulation kit. But with Sid's haphazard trucking schedule, there wasn't much point.

She knew this ache was irrational, that one of these days surely she would conceive again. But she wanted another child so badly.

Sid was the best thing that had ever happened to Marian. Her parents had divorced when she was young. Dad had remarried and moved to Sacramento, while Mom got caught up with her job, leaving her daughter with a series of housekeepers. That was one reason Marian wanted to stay home with her own children.

Her teen years had been difficult. Overweight in slenderness-obsessed Southern California, Marian had lingered on the outskirts of her friends' social lives. People liked her good-naturedness, but they didn't notice the woman inside.

Then Sid came along, and then, of course, little Lisa. Marian smiled to herself. What was her hurry to complete her family? She was wishing her life away, and it was too good a life for that.

No longer in a hurry for her happy ending to arrive, Marian went down the hall to kiss her sleeping daughter.

Chapter Seven

Through the swirl of voices around the Polo Lounge patio, Terry heard the splash of a diver cutting into the nearby pool. Where else but Southern California would one conduct business practically at poolside?

Legend had it that many a high-stakes deal had been cut in the bungalows here at the Beverly Hills Hotel, or around the tables at the garden-like Polo Lounge. Legendary names drifted through, hidden behind lush greenery, shielded by discreet waiters. Or so he imagined. Actually, most of the other diners looked like tourists, and they were probably wondering what was so important about *him*.

Terry looked up as Joe Lancer, his producer, slid into a chair opposite him. "Sorry I'm late." In a land of the gorgeous, Joe worked hard merely to look ordinary—lifts in his shoes, hair implants, contact lenses, Armani suits. He was still short, still rotund and still balding; he squinted, and his suits were perpetually wrinkled. Somehow those flaws made Terry like him more.

The producer glanced at a menu and tossed it aside. "I'll have the club sandwich. Restaurants always have a club sandwich."

"And a chopped salad." Terry prided himself on having picked up such tidbits, through judicious reading of trade newspapers such as the *Los Angeles Times*.

The whole issue of "power eating" in the movie business struck him as hilarious. Heads of studios chafed over who was given the best table at the latest hot restaurant. Insiders prided themselves on never having to look at a menu, on knowing to order the caesar salad or goat cheese pizza or whatever was the house specialty.

A bunch of grown-ups acting like little kids, he mused. No wonder he loved Hollywood.

As soon as their order was placed, Joe said, "Listen, we got a lot going. I'm gonna renew the option— I'll get back to your agent. I was hoping to do it last week, but I been swamped."

"Oh, sure." Terry's neck swiveled as Pia Zadora strolled by. At least, he thought it was Pia Zadora.

"Michael's out of town." Joe never used last names—Terry assumed Michael referred to Michael Douglas. "Kathleen doesn't look like a go. She's tied up with something at Disney. But listen, how about Holly?"

It took Terry a moment to figure out that Joe must mean Holly Hunter, but by that time the producer was rattling on. "I've got a coupla directors reading the treatment. Peter's tied up with some war thing in the Balkans, but maybe Oliver, you know? Or David, might be strange enough for him. Or Brian, there's a long shot."

Their food appeared just then, which gave Terry time to sort out Joe's rapid-fire information. Peter could mean either Peter Weir or Peter Bogdanovich; Oliver was Oliver Stone; David, he supposed, must be David Lynch, and of course Brian would be Brian De Palma.

He had a hard time believing all those directors would be interested in *Major League Vampire*. It was too offbeat.

"How about Penny?" he said, omitting the Marshall.

"Naw, naw, not her style," Joe mumbled through a mouthful of sandwich. "Listen, we want to get moving on this. I gotta get the elements attached to nail down the backers. Then I can start selling the foreign rights, video rights, cover the whole budget before we even shoot, you know?"

"Elements" meant stars or directors. They were the key to getting the project "green lighted," or approved, by the "money men." Sometimes Terry felt as if he'd fallen into a twilight zone where ordinary words took on strange and bizarre meanings.

Back to basics. "So you're renewing the option?" he said.

"Yeah, yeah. Gimme a few weeks." Joe nodded. "Start shooting by August, have a summer release next year." He waved to someone across the room. "Brandon, how ya doing?"

Terry peered over, but if Brandon Tartikoff was dining nearby, he was doing a good job of hiding. Sometimes Terry wondered if Joe made these things up.

It wasn't a pleasant thought. He decided not to dwell on it.

"So, great," Terry said.

"Yeah." Joe wiped his mouth with a heavy cloth napkin and tossed it on the table. "Gotta run. Good to see ya. You take care." He started off, then turned back. "Listen, that new book of yours. Have your agent send me the manuscript."

"I think he's waiting for page proofs," Terry said.

"I gotta see it sooner than that. Once it's in proofs, everybody in town'll be reading it. Okay? Super. You're looking great!"

Joe breezed out. At least he took the bill with him, Terry noted.

Meetings with Joe always left him with the feeling of having glimpsed a sumptuous buffet and been served an appetizer. Hungry not for food, but for... what? Glory? Maybe. Money? Not for its own sake, but for the sake of what it could buy.

He'd love to pay off Mitch's loan early. Then he'd buy Rose the biggest dollhouse ever assembled, and give Bopper a motorized kiddy car. He'd take them both to Disneyland, let them pick out any souvenir they wanted...

And Karen. What would Karen like?

Terry rested his chin in his palm, remembering how she'd looked last week in that shimmering blue dress. Now, be honest, he told himself. You're not really remembering how she *looked*.

How she felt. Yielding in his arms. Ready and eager, intensely female, romantic without a trace of coyness. Clear about what she wanted and ready to take it without apology.

He needed her with an intensity that surpassed the physical. It was new in his experience, which was reasonably varied for his thirty-two years. There were plenty of women, he'd found, who enjoyed the pleasures of his bed without wanting anything long-term. And he'd had exactly the same reaction to them.

Terry liked women. He enjoyed their honesty, their practicality, their appreciation of good music and good food. All those qualities seemed to peak in Karen, along with a warm earthiness that anchored him.

So why did he feel relieved that they hadn't become lovers, after all?

Terry didn't want to think about it. He hadn't wanted to think about it all week. But Joe had taken off and left him in the middle of lunch, all by himself, surrounded by tourists. He couldn't avoid thinking about it.

The truth was that making love with Karen would cement a bond Terry wasn't sure he could handle.

What was it that singled out one woman from all the others? Was it the shadows in her gray eyes? The warm silences that curled in the corners of her house? The fierce devotion she held like an umbrella over her children?

Something came alive in him when he felt her nearby. An ache to see that fierce devotion encompass him, too. A longing to slip inside those silences and banish those shadows.

Terry shuddered. Damn it, he was *falling*. Which was all right, as long as he could keep his attachment on the level of infatuation.

He'd thought for a long time that he was ready for something serious. For love. For marriage.

But Karen was so intensely real that he couldn't fool himself. The thought of tying off all the loose ends of his future and setting himself on one unswerving path scared the hell out of Terry.

Still, he thought, they could work it out. Enjoy each other, help each other. Make a home together for a while. Maybe a year or two. That wasn't so scary, was it? He could go on basically as he was, with Karen and her kids to share the good times.

He'd work on that.

"THIS WON'T DO IT." She hadn't heard George come out of his office until the computer-designed flier floated across Karen's desk. "You've got it all wrong. I want the square footage of the garage office included with the house. And that isn't a pool, it's a spa."

Karen bit back the retort that she'd only used the information he himself had provided. George wasn't good at accepting blame.

"Fine, I'll get these—"

"I want it in the mail tonight!" he added. "Tonight, Karen!" And headed for the door.

"The buyers on the Walnut property are coming in," she warned before he could disappear.

"Take care of it. I promised to pick up Bonnie at school today—my wife's busy with the garden club." George's words drifted back as he strode off.

Karen glanced at her watch. Four o'clock. She'd be here until six, at least. This was getting to be an old tape, and she hated it more every time George played it.

She had to figure out a way to get out of here before she turned into a snarling old witch, Karen told herself as she redesigned the flier.

When the door jangled, she didn't look up right away, assuming it was the buyers. She dug around in her desk for their papers, then looked up to see Terry's grin.

"Oh!" Karen couldn't help but smile. There was something infectious about his attitude toward life.

"Any chance of knocking off early?" Terry caught the grimace before it had passed her eyes. "I amend that. Could you use some help?"

"Oh, yes. Would you run down to the copy shop and get two hundred of these printed?" She handed him the flier. "I know it's a lot to ask but..."

"Aye, aye." He saluted and took off.

Karen began running off mailing labels and sticking them on envelopes. Terry arrived back just as the young couple stalked through the doorway.

"I really don't see why we had to leave work early to sign something we already signed once," the husband grumbled.

"I agree with you," Karen said. "These escrow officers, some of them..."

Then it hit her. She needed a notary public to put a seal on the signatures and George, who was one, had left. She shot a helpless glance at Terry.

"What?" He plopped the pile of fliers onto her desk. "What what?"

She told him. The buyers watched with justifiable indignation.

"No problem." Terry pointed across the parking lot. "There's a bank over there. They must have a notary."

"Yes, but that's not *our* bank," Karen said.

"I'll handle it." He collected the papers and escorted the buyers out the door. The last thing she heard him say was, "You're buying your first house, huh? Does it have a fireplace?"

At least tempers had been soothed for a little while.

Her fingers itched from folding and stuffing by the time Terry came bouncing back. "All done!" He held up the completed papers. "Want me to drop these somewhere?"

"Yes!" Karen gazed at him as if she were an explorer who'd just discovered the Fountain of Youth. "*Would* you?"

He took the address of the escrow company and out he went.

At five-fifteen, she stuffed the last envelope into the mailbox in front of the office. Terry's dragon pulled to the curb with a resounding ooga-ooga.

"I'll get the food, you get the kids." he called. She nodded, and watched the wagon's tail wiggle away.

Knowing Terry was like being friends with a whirlwind, Karen mused as she headed for Marian's house. With his help and his gee-whiz enthusiasm, he'd banished her grumpiness and infused a little of his energy into her veins.

Too bad the American Medical Association didn't know about Terry. They'd make him the prescription of choice for depression.

Dinner was consumed in a merry clatter of dishes highlighted by childish voices. Terry elaborated, to humorous effect, on his lunch in Beverly Hills. Karen could visualize the pool and the palm trees, the outdoor tables filled with tourists, the woman with spike heels and chipmunk cheeks who might or might not have been Pia Zadora, the movie executive that only Joe Lancer could see.

"It's like a cast of characters from a movie," she told him as the children popped off to the den.

"I fantasize sometimes about being famous myself," he admitted. "Having people come up and ask for my autograph. Something like that happened once."

"Really?" She couldn't imagine anyone wanting her signature on anything but a check.

"I was at the theater—the Ahmanson—and a lady burbled right up to me in the aisle and said, 'Aren't you Terry Vogel? The author?' I ducked my head modestly and admitted that I was. And she said, 'Oh, I met you at my daughter's Halloween party. We loved your costume!'"

Karen chuckled. "But Marian had heard of you. You *are* famous. Just think, someday producers will go to the Polo Lounge and pretend *you're* sitting at another table waving to them."

It was his turn to laugh. "Even so!" He sipped coffee from his take-out cup. He'd been thoughtful enough to buy some, which Karen had discreetly poured out and replaced with homemade. Even instant was better than the tinny brew. "Hey, this isn't bad. They've improved."

She admitted the truth.

Terry shook his head. "You have a knack for these little touches that make such a difference. I don't know how you do it."

"It's hardly a talent like yours," Karen protested.

"But the art of everyday life, that's something I never mastered." He stared deep into the creamy liquid. "I've told you my dreams. Your turn."

Before she could talk further, she needed to check on the children. Her ears picked up the click of Bopper's blocks and the murmur of Rose's voice as she played with a doll. Amazing how easy it was to keep track of kids by their noises.

"What I'd like," she said, "is to take some college classes. Office management, that kind of thing. So I can move up. I want a job with advancement possibilities."

"Why not start now?" Terry said. "You want it, go for it."

Karen nodded toward the other room. "With the house payment, I could never have afforded a baby-sitter. I guess I could now, but it's hard to find someone you can count on in the evenings. Teenagers have a way of canceling out. They're okay for once in a while, but I'd hate to depend on them every week."

"What about Marian?" He shot a look toward the kitchen, and Karen found she could read his thoughts.

"We're out of cookies, but there's some peanut-butter crackers." She waited while he fetched them. How could a man eat so much and never gain weight? Maybe the answer was the rowing machine he'd placed in the middle of his bedroom, with the claim that it was modern art. He must use the thing sometime, but Karen had never caught him.

When he'd settled back at the dining-room table, she said, "I couldn't impose on Marian more than I already do. As it is, I try to watch Lisa for her occasionally but it would take a hundred years to pay her back. Not that she's asking."

Terry downed a couple of crackers. "I could help out once in a while," he said. "If the baby-sitter didn't show up."

Karen knew she ought to jump at the offer. Was she simply too proud to accept Terry's help? Or was she heeding a little warning voice inside that said she shouldn't depend on him too much?

"We could...talk about it," she was saying when the phone rang.

Karen took the call in the kitchen. Her "Hello?" brought a momentary silence. Finally an elderly woman queried, "Is this the residence of Terence Vogel?"

"Yes, it is. Just a moment, please."

Terry looked puzzled when informed that an old lady had asked for him. "Perhaps one of my many fans," he said as he claimed the phone.

Cleaning up in the dining room, Karen tried not to listen, but there was no mistaking the tension that clipped Terry's words.

Phrases jumped out—"I have no intention of explaining," and "she lives here, that's all I care to say." Uh-oh. Apparently he'd landed in trouble because Karen had answered the phone.

But his grandmother, she knew, had been dead for several years. Who else could provoke such a response?

When Terry stalked out of the kitchen, he quivered with indignation. Karen caught him looking around as if for something to pummel.

"The rowing machine," she said.

"Right." He took the stairs two at a time.

The thump-thump of the machine lasted right through Rose and Bopper's bedtime. They asked for Terry several times, and Karen realized how accustomed they'd all become to sharing this nightly ritual with him.

"Terry's not feeling too great," she said. "I'm sure he'll be in later to kiss you good night."

"But I'll be asleep!" Bopper protested.

"Then you can dream that he comes in and kisses you." She tucked her son under the covers.

"I won't go to sleep," the little boy said. "I'll stay awake all night." His eyelids fluttered.

In her room, Rose clutched her doll tightly but didn't say anything.

Karen stroked her daughter's hair. "Terry's not mad at us, you know," she said.

"But he won't stay." Rose nuzzled her doll.

"He's a friend." Karen tried to keep her tone neutral. "Sometimes friendships last forever, and sometimes people grow apart. But that's not what's bothering Terry tonight. He had an argument with someone and it made him angry. He's going to a lot of trouble not to take it out on us."

"I wish he would," Rose said. "If we could all yell at each other . . . I don't like people keeping secrets."

"It's not a secret." Karen kissed her. "I'll bet he'll tell you all about it tomorrow."

"I guess so." Rose rolled over to face the wall.

Karen stopped outside Terry's door. She didn't want to intrude, but perhaps by now he'd worked off the main force of his fury.

She rapped lightly and cracked the door ajar. "I could make popcorn." Food was usually the way to Terry's heart.

"Push some under the door."

"I will not!"

"Then I guess I'll have to come down."

He arrived in the kitchen as the fluffy kernels were mounding in the popper. Karen retrieved a saucer of melted margarine and Terry located the saltshaker.

For a while all Karen heard was the crunch of popcorn as they sat side by side.

Finally . . .

"That was Great-Aunt Elinora," Terry said. "Grandma's sister."

Karen risked annoying him by saying, "Couldn't you just have told her I'm your tenant?"

"I wouldn't mind if she were merely curious." He exhaled deeply. "I wouldn't even mind if she were a little shocked. But the way she puts things, it's as if she had a right to order my life around, and how dare I do anything without her permission. This is my great-aunt, whom I haven't seen in five years!"

"Doesn't she have kids of her own?" Karen ventured.

"She drives them crazy, too." Terry propped his feet on an empty chair. "She lives in Boston. Her son moved to Seattle years ago, and her daughter's gone all the way to Italy. It's as if they couldn't get far enough."

"How sad." Karen thought about how much she wished her own mother hadn't moved even forty miles away.

"I know I should have more sympathy for an old lady," Terry said. "Especially since she's a member of my family. But she has this way, when I'm talking with her, of twisting a knife in my stomach. Making me feel like a little boy who can't do anything right. I resent her assuming the worst about you!"

"She doesn't know me," Karen pointed out. "I know it's none of my business, but wouldn't it be easier if you learned not to take her so seriously?"

"Yes," Terry said. "Now how do I do that?"

Karen had no answers. She certainly hadn't figured out a way to distance herself from Bobby yet. Even the information that he'd called Marian last month had roused her to sheer fury. "I wish I knew."

"I guess..." Terry mumbled between the last remnants of popcorn "...I guess it pushes my buttons when someone acts as if they own me. As if I were a thing, a stick figure to fit into a prearranged pattern, instead of a person with a life of my own."

"I don't see how anybody could make that mistake." Karen smiled, and to her relief he smiled back.

"You cheer me up."

"Turnabout's fair play." She dug around in the bowl for one of the remaining half-popped morsels, and her fingers brushed Terry's. They both stopped breathing for a second.

"We're not going to pursue this, are we?" he murmured.

"Not while you're so keyed up." Karen withdrew her hand. "Your great-aunt really got to you."

"I'll clean up in here." He hopped up. "Go away. Stop tempting me, you jezebel."

"I know how helpless you become in the grip of your passions," she said.

"If you don't cut it out, I'll put on some music," he threatened. "Ever waltz with a man who has butter on his fingers?"

"Okay, okay." She pushed back her chair. "Don't forget to kiss Bopper. He threatened to wait up."

"I won't forget."

THE LITTLE BOY slept curled around his teddy bear. Terry planted a kiss on his soft cheek, then kissed the teddy bear for good measure.

Rose was still awake. "You can yell at me," she whispered.

"What for?"

"Just... because I'm here." Tears shone in her round dark eyes.

He kissed the tip of her nose. "I like that you're here. And I don't feel like yelling at you."

"I'd rather hear you yelling than have you go away," she said.

He scooped the little girl into his arms. "I'm not going anywhere. Rose, you're not responsible for everything that happens around you. If I'm in a bad mood sometimes, it's not because of you. I may not always be available right when you want me, but I'll come as soon as I can."

"It scares me when you're not here," she said.

He held Rose close and hoped she wouldn't notice the tears rimming his eyes. He wasn't sure he could explain them, even to himself. "I love you," he said at last, and tucked her in.

In his own room, Terry glared at the rowing machine. Thanks to it, he was going to ache tomorrow. Maybe he should just take the day off and go borrow Mitch's spa. Right. As if he needed an excuse to get out of working!

Actually, he loved the way *Dream a Little Scream of Me* was developing. And he had a great idea for a new character, a snotty social climber who was about to meet her Valhalla.

Even after he'd brushed his teeth and changed into his pajamas, though, Terry couldn't sleep. Part of his restlessness had to do with Karen. And knowing that she lay sleeping right down the hall didn't help.

Neither did the nagging suspicion that he'd been rude to a lonely if cranky old lady.

Sure, Great-Aunt Elinora had been rude to him first, but that was one of the prerogatives of old age. As far as her manipulative bossiness, she'd paid a heavy price for it. Terry knew her far-flung children rarely visited.

She'd only called Terry in the first place to wish him good luck in his new home. Maybe hoping for a little chitchat to warm her January night.

It was too late to call her back, so Terry dug around in his desk until he found a box of stationery.

He sat for an hour, writing the funniest apology he could think of. He enclosed photographs of Karen's children and filled the note with anecdotes. It was as close as he could come to giving Great-Aunt Elinora the cosy chat he hadn't provided in person.

When he was finished he wasn't angry anymore. There was the answer to Karen's question about how to put distance between yourself and someone who bugged you: use your sense of humor.

He hoped Great-Aunt Elinora had one.

Chapter Eight

Karen knew there was going to be trouble when she came downstairs the next morning and found Bopper sitting at the kitchen table wearing an oversize shirt of his father's.

The little boy nearly disappeared beneath a tent of paint-smeared fabric, which he wore backward like a smock. Bobby had given it to him years before to encourage him to take up painting, a hobby that Bopper had approached with all the enthusiasm and lack of staying power of a toddler.

Bobby hadn't understood why his son quickly abandoned his paints for a tricycle. He'd sulked all day.

Karen avoided commenting on the shirt as she went about making breakfast.

The last time Bopper had dragged it out was right after Bobby left, slumping around in it as if he'd put on mourning.

She had a suspicion he'd brought it out again because of Terry's failure to appear for the nightly tuck-in ritual. Perhaps a special treat of pancakes would restore Bopper's good humor. The trick was to keep his mind off the shirt and his reasons for wearing it.

She'd forgotten about Rose.

"Oh, Bopper!" Rose cried when she appeared in the doorway, before Karen could signal her to silence. "You're not fretting about Daddy again!"

Bopper stared into his cup.

"Honey," Karen warned.

"You're just like him," Rose told her brother. "Sulking! Because you're not the first, last and foremost thing in Terry's life!"

"He didn't kiss me good-night." Bopper blew angry bubbles into his milk.

"Did, too, only you fell asleep." Rose kissed her mother and sat down. "I know because he came in to see me, so he must have stopped off to see you, too."

"Well, he should have come at bedtime." Bopper glared at the plate of pancakes Karen set in front of him. "I don't want any."

"I do!" Rose reached for hers eagerly.

Bopper toyed with his food. He was so stubborn that one Halloween he'd refused to eat dinner, even though it meant he wasn't allowed to go trick-or-treating. He had decided it was unfair to have to eat anything other than candy, so he ended up eating nothing at all. That, Karen supposed, was what people meant by cutting off your nose to spite your face.

She hoped Terry might appear to smooth things over, but he didn't. At least Bopper sneaked a few forkfuls of pancake when he thought she wasn't looking. Five-year-olds never figured out that moms could tell all they needed from what was left on the plate.

Sherlock Holmes had probably learned most of his tricks from his mother, she reflected.

"You're not going to wear that thing to kindergarten, are you?" Rose demanded.

"Why not?" Bopper planted his elbows on the table.

"Your friends will think it's silly."

"She's right." Karen was well aware that five-year-olds functioned like mini-teenagers, with an acute sensitivity to the opinions of their peers. "You know how Vinnie and Andy like to tease."

"Who cares?"

Bopper defiantly wore the shirt all the way out to the car, then took it off. "I don't want to get it dirty," he said.

Karen took them over to Marian's, where they would catch the school bus a half hour later. She'd tried to get George to shift his opening time, since no clients ever came in at eight o'clock anyway, but he wouldn't consider it. Of course, he himself rarely arrived before nine.

Her sister-in-law managed to look cheerful and wide-awake even at this hour. "Why the gloom?" she asked Bopper, who had stuffed his shirt under one arm.

"Where's Lisa?" He dashed past his aunt.

"He's mad because Terry didn't come kiss him at bedtime." Rose made a face. "He's such a baby!" She strode into the house with queenly grace.

Marian looked at Karen.

"I suppose it is hard on Bopper," she admitted. "I mean, having Terry in the house, when he's not really part of the family. Maybe I shouldn't wait till summer to move."

"Come have coffee." Marian waved her inside.

Karen glanced guiltily at her watch. Well, she could afford to be a few minutes late.

While the children planted themselves in front of "Sesame Street," she told Marian about last night's conversation, how she'd mentioned her dream of going back to school and Terry had volunteered to watch the children, but only on a standby basis.

"He always keeps part of himself in reserve," she concluded.

"You two." Marian tapped her fingers together. "Dancing around each other. Karen, a guy like that— he needs a push. Anyone can see he's crazy about you. But he's not going to take the next step of his own accord. He's gun-shy."

"I won't box him in," Karen said. "Then he'd be justified in leaving the way Bobby did. It has to come from inside him. And I have to feel absolutely certain that he's committed."

"You have a point," her sister-in-law admitted. "Still, I feel like he's teetering on the edge, and once he jumped off, he'd never turn back."

Karen told her about the great-aunt who'd tried to control Terry with her disapproval. "He can't stand feeling that he's being locked into somebody else's expectations. Trying to tie him down would be the worst thing I could do."

"Maybe," Marian conceded. "I hope he doesn't protect himself out of a life."

"Thanks for the coffee and sympathy." Karen handed back her cup. "I don't know where I'd be without you, Marian."

"Your life is better than a soap opera," her sister-in-law said. "I wouldn't miss it."

It was nearly eight-thirty when Karen pulled into her parking space. Her heart dropped when she saw George's Cadillac already parked.

Wouldn't you know he'd pick today to come in early?

There was no one in the outer office when she entered. Glumly Karen revved up the office coffeepot and started her computer.

She was pulling out her list of things to do when George emerged from his sanctum.

"Well?" he said.

Karen debated pretending not to understand but decided that would only irritate him. "I'm sorry I was late."

"My realtors' breakfast was canceled, so I came in at seven-thirty," George said. "Half an hour ago I received an important call. A come-list-me from an owner I've been talking with for months. A half-million-dollar property in La Habra Heights."

"That's great," Karen said.

"I don't think he'd have been too happy talking to my answering machine." George blew his nose. Whenever he got angry, his allergies acted up.

"George..."

"I pay you to be here at eight o'clock."

"That's right!" Karen flared. "Eight to five, isn't it? And what time do you think I left here last night?"

"That isn't the point..."

She hadn't meant to start an argument, but she couldn't let this go. "What is the point, George? That I'm paid by the hour? In that case, you owe me for a couple hundred hours of overtime."

"I pay you to get a job done," he said quickly.

"Fine!" She slammed a file on her desk. "Then let me do it!"

George shifted from one foot to the other and then went back into his office.

Karen glared at his door hard enough to pierce holes in it. The nerve of that man! Slave driver was too kind a term for him.

She made up her mind at that moment to take at least one college course this year. She wasn't sure how much longer she could tolerate George, paycheck or no paycheck.

How a doddering old woman in her nineties could make Mrs. Abraham Bundy so angry, the society matron had yet to figure out.

She sat now, most unwillingly, across from old Gladys Maycap in the run-down Victorian living room.

Outdated, that was what this house was. Along with its gnarly, pinch-faced occupant.

Mrs. Maycap poured a cup of tea and added two lumps of sugar without asking. "I under-stand you told the board I wasn't suitable to sit on the fashion show committee," the old lady said.

"We're seeking people a bit more au courant with the haut monde," Mrs. Bundy said.

"When it comes to style," the old woman sneered, "it's hardly something one picks up by marrying money."

"I beg your pardon!"

"Come here." Gladys stood up imperiously. "There's something I want to show you. Some-thing in my closet.

Terry fought back the urge to cackle and rub his hands together. What a surprise awaited that nou-veau-riche snob Mrs. Bundy!

Not that he had a lot of sympathy for her tormentor, either. He saved his sympathy for the novel's heroine, Bridget Weintraub, a venetian blind saleswoman with an innocent nature and remarkable courage.

What she needed was a love interest. Terry generally avoided generating a romantic subplot—they tended to turn sappy. But Bridget deserved the best.

Stretching out in his desk chair, Terry thought about last night's discussion with Karen. Why did he hesitate to promise one evening a week to watch the children? He'd really missed reading their bedtime story last night.

He knew it had nothing to do with Bopper or Rose— or with Karen, either. It was one of those gut feelings, a creeping tension that started in the chest and sneaked into his throat. As if someone were tightening a noose.

That gave him an idea for how the Thing-in-the-Closet could dispose of Betsy Bundy. Terry's hands were poised over his keyboard when the phone rang.

He nearly let the answering machine pick it up. But it might be his agent—or Joe Lancer—so he took it.

"Terry? Becky Reynolds!" His New York editor spoke mostly in exclamation points.

"Becky! Good to hear your voice." But he wasn't sure he meant it. Sometimes editors called with good news—an excellent review, an unusually big foreign sale—but more often they wanted another rewrite or...

"You know, we'd talked about putting *Ghoul of the Golden West* on our winter list?" In fact, Becky had told him without any qualifications that the book would be their lead Christmas title.

"Talked about?" He already suspected what was coming.

"We just found out Stephen King and Peter Straub both have big titles due the same month," Becky went on. "So, this is even better! We're moving you to the spring list!"

That meant a publication delay of three months. It meant missing the Christmas shopping season. It meant that royalties, which were paid out semiannually following publication, would be delayed, too.

"Am I still a lead title?" Terry ventured.

"Of course!" Becky glowed with enthusiasm, as always. He'd met her only once, on a publicity trip to New York for his previous book. She'd turned out to be a short, lively woman in her late twenties. Her smooth page boy bounced when she smiled, retreated behind her ears when she concentrated and flopped into her eyes when she turned evasive. Terry wondered what the hair was doing now.

"Do you mind my asking what kind of promotion you've got planned?" he said. "Have I been assigned a publicist yet?"

"It's a little early for that!" Becky said. "But it's got such terrific potential! The western setting—the satire—we just love your sense of humor!"

"Thank you." Why did Terry have the feeling the hair was flopping into her eyes?

"Gotta go!" Becky chortled. "Good to talk to you!"

"You, too." He settled the phone into its cradle.

What if...

Terry rarely dwelled on the negative, but a tiny feather of doubt tickled the edges of his brain. What if the book wasn't given a special promotion? He would still earn enough to cover his normal expenses, but...

Joe Lancer had mentioned renewing the option, but he hadn't done it yet. And renewing wasn't the same as picking up. The option on *Major League Vampire* had only gone for ten thousand dollars, and a renewal would bring even less. If it were picked up, Terry would be richer to the tune of a hundred and fifty thousand dollars. If . . .

For a terrifying instant, he confronted the possibility that both his film deal and his much anticipated breakthrough onto the bestseller lists might founder.

Where the hell was he going to come up with the money to pay Mitch back?

He couldn't let himself think about what Karen might say. But this whole line of speculation was preposterous. After all, his agent would soon be sending copies of *Golden West* to producers, so he'd have a shot at a new movie sale.

In a month or two, *Dream a Little Scream* would be finished, as well. There were infinite possibilities. The money would roll in from somewhere.

BOPPER WAS WEARING Bobby's shirt again, when Karen picked the children up. He stared, as if defying her to comment, so she didn't.

"We're having spaghetti," she announced in the car before anyone could ask.

"No onions!" Bopper said.

"I never use onions," Karen reminded him.

"And no zucchini, either!" Rose warned.

Last summer Karen's garden had yielded a supply of tomatoes barely adequate for her ravenous family, but enough zucchini for the entire Army of the Potomac. She'd tried chopping it, grating it, and adding it to any recipe in which it might even vaguely fit. No wonder the kids had gotten sick of it.

"No zucchini," she said, and refrained from reminding them that summer squash didn't grow in the winter.

Cooking a meal with two hungry children nagging at her ankles wasn't Karen's idea of a good time, but she'd set out the ingredients before leaving this morning. She only had to flick on the burner under the pot of water, stick the sauce in the microwave and...

She'd scarcely opened the front door when she smelled it, the unmistakable aroma of tomato sauce and basil.

"Terry!" said Rose.

Bopper glowered. "He prob'ly uses onions."

Rose dashed into the kitchen. Karen heard her say in surprise, "Oh. Hello."

"Hi, there, young lady!" came the voice of Terry's writer friend, Joni Rodd.

"Puppies!" Bopper raced after his sister.

No puppies, Karen prayed silently as she followed. On damp days, the living room still emitted a faint doggy odor as a result of their Christmas encounter.

She was relieved to find Joni in the kitchen with only the children for company. Spaghetti boiled on the stove, and Joni was chopping tomatoes for a salad.

"I'm baby-sitting," she explained.

"You are?" Karen searched her memory. "I don't..."

Terry popped in from the backyard, carrying a hammer and nails. "That storage shed is a mess!" He stowed his gear and washed his hands. "Bopper, my friend! Did you know you snore? I went to kiss you last night and you blasted me into another dimension!"

Bopper bit his lip.

"He's sulking," Rose said.

"Am not!" The little boy hugged himself, which meant he was hugging his father's shirt as well. "I don't even care."

"Who sets the table?" Terry aimed a grin at Karen.

"Me." Rose opened the silverware drawer.

"Me, too!" Bopper raced to get down the napkins, nearly tripping over his oversize shirt. He shrugged it off and tossed it aside, his moodiness forgotten.

As they were eating, Terry explained Joni's presence. "My friend Mitch invited you and me to a late-night swimming party at his house. A very intimate swimming party, just four of us. Mitch loves to go to parties, but he hardly ever has anyone over."

"If it's a party, maybe I'd better not eat much." Karen stared hungrily at the oversize portion she'd taken. She'd hate to spoil her appetite for tasty hors d'oeuvres.

"Mitch's refreshments are likely to be of the liquid variety," Terry assured her.

"Take advantage of the situation," Joni said. "Mitch has a gorgeous pool."

"I don't understand why he's doing this." Karen tapped some parmesan onto her pasta.

"Want a guess?" Joni was already digging into seconds. "He's met a new lady. He wants to show her around the house without making her think he has designs."

"What kind of designs?" asked Rose.

"Magic designs." Terry pretended to weave a spell with his hands.

"I'm coming, too!" Bopper declared.

"I was just kidding," Terry said quickly.

"I don't care. I love to swim. You can't leave me here!"

"Bopper," Joni said. "I came all this way just to play with you and your sister. You wanna make me cry?"

He nodded.

"Later," Joni said.

Karen decided it would be all right to go to Mitch's, but she only ate half her spaghetti. She didn't want to bulge out of her swimsuit.

MITCH'S HOUSE SAT atop a hill at the end of a narrow, winding road. A modern split-level, it boasted a sparkling view of city lights.

They parked in the drive and walked up. The front door stood ajar.

"They're probably out back." Terry walked in and called, "Mitch? You here?"

He led the way through a wide marble-floored hallway. Karen glimpsed a well-equipped kitchen toward the front of the house; the living room, conversely, was at the back. The whole interior, with its cathedral ceilings and rooms that flowed into each other, had been built for entertaining. The low-key decor might be a bit too calculated for Karen's taste, but it could easily have graced the pages of a magazine.

Not a toy in sight. No apple juice stains marred the creamy carpet. The tabletops flaunted displays of etched glass and porcelain figures.

Karen sighed.

They stepped out a rear door onto the highest of a series of terraces leading down to the swimming pool. The spa, she noticed, was located off to their right, on a middle-level terrace; beyond the pool rose a gazebo, overlooking a steep drop to what must be a valley, but the electric lights didn't penetrate its depths.

"It looks like a movie star's home," she murmured.

Below them, Mitch stood chest-deep in water, smoking a pipe while a young woman with dark hair cut laps through the water.

He seemed relieved to see them. "Ho, there!" Mitch lifted his pipe in salute.

Karen did her best to descend the terrace steps gracefully. It was a task made difficult by their uneven heights and lengths. You wouldn't want to walk down here carrying a tray of drinks, she reflected.

But you wouldn't have to, because the drinks were already set up on a bar at poolside. Joni had been right. The only food in sight was a bowl of pretzels.

The young woman burst from the water, flipping droplets from her hair. She was strikingly pretty, in her early twenties.

"Hi." She smiled, more at ease than Karen would have expected. "I'm Sally."

They exchanged greetings. Then Sally said, "I hope you don't mind if I get in my laps. I just love to swim." She dove under the water.

"You didn't tell me you had a date with a mermaid." Terry shrugged off his T-shirt.

"Didn't realize it myself." Mitch chewed grumpily at the pipe stem. "We've hardly exchanged two words."

"'I love to swim' is four words." Despite her light tone, Karen felt uncomfortable, slipping off her wrap skirt and knit top in front of him, but there was no cabana in sight. And after all, underneath it she *was* wearing a modest one-piece swimsuit.

She removed her clothing to find the air crisp but not too chilly. In Southern California, the days were usually warm in winter, but the temperatures dropped by as much as thirty degrees at night. "I hope the water's heated."

Terry slid in. "Nice and toasty."

"Couldn't stand it otherwise," Mitch grumbled, his eye on Sally as she chopped across the pool. "Isn't she done yet?"

Karen had to chuckle. Sally clearly had an independent mind.

They discussed the day's news events until Sally swam up, twisted water from her hair and helped herself to a beer.

"Something about the air up here," she said. "It's really clear."

"Smoggy as hell," Mitch muttered.

"You're in a mood, aren't you?" Not at all fazed, she turned to Karen. "Are you a writer, too?"

"Not me. Terry."

Sally began quizzing Terry about his books, and was thrilled to discover she'd read one of them. She proceeded to interrogate Mitch and Terry about their writing techniques and where they got their ideas.

"Out of *Ladies' Home Journal*," Mitch growled. He was missing no opportunity to take his ill temper out on his date. Karen wondered how such a surly character managed to appeal to such an attractive young woman, but Sally appeared fascinated by authors.

"I get ideas from everywhere," Terry said. "The problem isn't getting them, it's developing them."

"But you hear about the concept being everything," Sally pressed. "Like how some movie studio paid a million dollars for a one-line summary. I could come up with ideas if they'd pay me that kind of money.''

"You and me both," Mitch said.

"That idea was probably worth a million dollars because it came from Sidney Sheldon, who knew how to turn it into a bestselling novel and a miniseries," Terry pointed out. "Ideas are a dime a dozen. Execution is everything."

Sally grimaced. "I always figured I'd write a book someday. I just don't have time."

"I was working at an ad agency when I wrote my first novel," Terry said. "I didn't have a lot of spare time, but I made myself set aside an hour a day."

"When would I exercise?" Sally challenged. "Honestly!"

Mitch released an exasperated grunt. Karen guessed that when he'd invited them over, he hadn't expected Sally to take such an interest in group discussion.

"Where did you two meet?" she asked.

"At a book signing." Sally downed the dregs of her beer.

"She's a book groupie," Mitch said.

"We can always use more readers." Terry rested one arm around Karen's waist. The swish of the water carried her leg against his.

"I collect authors," Sally agreed. "But I don't get to visit their houses very often."

"I should have invited you on the Charity Tour of Homes." Mitch's voice had taken a sarcastic edge.

"Well, I'm done swimming." Sally hefted herself out of the pool. "Mitch, you coming?"

"Where?" He puffed at his pipe, which had gone out.

"You promised to show me the manuscript you're working on," she said. "I'd like to talk about how you develop your characters."

Mitch nearly dropped his pipe in his hurry to get out. "Really?"

Sally was halfway up the steps by the time Mitch reached her. They walked the rest of the way together.

"She's got him hopping." Karen smiled. "I think he likes her, although he doesn't always act like it."

"He's not the most patient man in the world," Terry said, and Karen choked back the laughter.

They swam lazily through the warm water. After Sally's grilling Terry didn't seem to feel like talking, and neither did Karen.

She floated on her back, staring up at the night sky. Here in the heights there were few lights to distract from the stars. Karen wished she knew more about constellations, then was glad she didn't. Stars were too beautiful, remote and tantalizing, to categorize.

"Ever wonder if there's life up there?" Terry dog-paddled beside her.

"There ought to be." A welter of images flicked through her mind, from countless movies. "But I doubt if they look like giant insects, or people with bulbs on their heads. I wish we could know, without actually having contact."

"Some people think we *have* had contact," he mused.

"Do you?"

"There's a theory about flying saucers," Terry said. "That they're time machines from the future, piloted by history students doing research for their dissertations."

"Makes you feel small, doesn't it?" The water buoyed Karen from her heels to the roots of her hair. A lightness pervaded her, in spirit as well as in body. The cares that loomed so large in her ordinary life dwindled here.

They swam for a while longer. Terry's occasional paddling sent miniwaves lapping at Karen's sides, caressing her shoulders and legs.

She noticed a light switch on upstairs. "Is that his office?"

"He calls it the library." Terry stood up. "Let's try the whirlpool."

They dashed through air that had turned freezing, at least to wet bathers. A shock of intense warmth ushered them into the Jacuzzi. Terry turned on the jets, and they were cocooned in a private world of rushing water.

From here, Karen realized, you couldn't see any other houses. She liked the sense of being entirely secluded and yet out beneath the open sky.

Terry reclined opposite, his long legs tangling with hers. Karen could feel the curve of his knees, the soft pressure of his toes against her thigh.

She tried not to acknowledge the excitement that bubbled inside. If she lay here quietly, if she didn't look at him, they could both escape facing the rush of urgency that surely was tingling through his nerve endings as forcefully as hers.

Steam surged in her veins and the last of her tensions melted away. There was no sensation but the gentle stroking of Terry's legs against hers and this blossoming hunger, this pleasant, aching need to be filled and filled again.

Karen didn't dare move. She couldn't open her eyes.

His fingers found one of her ankles, exploring the edges of the bones and the sensitive pressure points above the heel. He was only giving her a massage. There was nothing wrong with lying here, desire shimmering up her legs, enjoying a foot massage.

Who was she kidding?

Karen looked up to see Terry watching her. "We could take this either of two ways," he said. "We could go home now or we could stay."

In the shelter of steam and tumbling water, they could slip from their suits as easily as two seals tumbling over each other. They could float hip against hip, their bodies creating a new reality as old as the stars themselves. They could bring this passionate flood to a natural, torrential release, fire upon the water, and pretend that they'd only been seduced by the night.

Karen bit her lip until it hurt. "We'd better leave," she said.

"I think so, too."

It was hard to get out, to hear the silence that washed down when Terry turned off the jets.

Karen looked up at the second-story window. It was still lit.

She wondered how much a young woman like Sally really had in common with Mitch. But perhaps her vigor and enthusiasm were exactly what he needed.

"Ready?" Terry, his T-shirt clinging damply to his chest, held out her clothes.

Karen wrapped on the skirt. "Ready." She fluffed a hand through her hair.

They walked silently back through the house. She felt him vibrating beside her with an unfulfilled longing that matched her own.

They couldn't keep this up forever. Karen vowed to avoid such situations in the future. Only a few months remained until summer.

On the way home, she gazed out the window at the stars. From the car, they appeared smaller and colder, dwindling like the last defiant traces of heat in her blood.

Chapter Nine

On Saturday, Karen had planned to spend the morning catching up on housework. She sometimes suspected that in the middle of the night, as she snoozed upstairs, elephants with muddy feet came dancing across the kitchen linoleum.

How else to explain this mess? she wondered as she stood, still in her robe, surveying the scuffed and spotted floor.

With an inward groan, she set to making coffee and laying out the breakfast dishes.

Bopper dragged into the kitchen a few minutes later wearing Bobby's old shirt. He lay down on the smudged linoleum and covered himself with his favorite blanket.

"Bops!" She sat beside him. "What's the matter?"

"I'm going to lie here till Daddy comes home." He peered up with tear-starred eyes.

"What brought this on?"

He tugged the blanket over his head.

"You must have had a bad dream." Karen stroked a defiant shock of her son's hair. "Want to tell me?"

The hair shook "no."

"Maybe you could do something with Terry this morning," she suggested.

"He always sleeps late."

Karen fended off a wave of irritation at his refusal to be soothed. It wasn't Bopper's fault she needed her morning cup of coffee. "How about some toast with peanut butter and grape jelly? Then you could get out your toy vacuum and help me clean house."

The hair shook again.

Rose padded through the door, kissed her mother distractedly and flopped into a chair. She didn't seem to notice her brother curled on the floor.

"I'm bored," she said.

Karen let out a long breath. There was no way she could clean the house with these two moping and whining under her feet. It wasn't fair to the children, and it wouldn't be fair to her, either.

"We could go to the park." She counted out eggs to scramble.

After a brief pause Bopper said, "Which park?"

"Parnell." The park, located on the east side of Whittier, featured a small petting zoo.

"Okay," her son said.

"I hate Parnell Park," Rose grumbled.

These were the times that tried a mother's inventiveness, if not her soul. "We could get out the camera Grandma Helene gave you for your birthday," she told her daughter. "You could take pictures of the animals."

Rose thought this over. "All right."

Karen had finished fixing the eggs before she saw that Bopper had left. She assumed he was getting dressed, until she heard a series of heavy thumps coming down the stairs.

Through the dining room, she spotted Terry and Bopper, jumping from step to step.

Terry grinned when he caught sight of her. "I'm coming to see the animals." With sleep-tossed hair falling across his forehead and a pair of rumpled Ninja Turtles pajamas, he looked like an overgrown kid himself.

"A day at the zoo." Karen ducked into the kitchen and tried not to notice the dark streaks that some roller-skating kangaroo had added to the floor while her back was turned.

"I'M THE KING OF everything!" Bopper cried from the heights of his fortress.

"And I am the Dark Knight!" Terry tossed him a stick and wielded one of his own. *"En garde!"*

"What's that mean?"

"Sword fight!"

Leaning back on the bench Karen watched the two figures, one tall and lanky, the other small and intense, hop back and forth. The child-sized fort was Bopper's favorite feature of the whole park. Amazing how a simple platform could blossom into an elaborate castle in a child's mind.

And a grown-up's, too, judging by Terry.

He was enjoying the fencing match as much as the five-year-old. "Take that, you blackguard!" Terry clutched his arm. "Oh, foul fiend! Thou hast stricken me!"

"There's more where that came from!" Bopper sliced the air with his stick.

The weather had turned overcast, and the park wasn't crowded. Rose wandered about, frowning into her viewfinder and training the little camera first on a pigeon, then on a woman pushing a stroller. Karen suspected she hadn't pressed the button more than a few times all morning.

Rose was a perfectionist. She wouldn't shoot unless she'd framed the shot just right. She'd snapped the llama when he stared directly at her, but the goats wouldn't move into the right positions and Rose had passed them by.

Karen liked to see her daughter take such care, but she hoped Rose wasn't becoming too compulsive to enjoy the ragged edges of life. This rigidity had become more pronounced since Bobby left. Perhaps it was the child's way of taking control over the helplessness she must have felt.

All the same it made her proud to watch Rose scrutinize a sparrow, step back to get the right angle and then shoot. Her daughter possessed a patience rare for her age and an artistic sense that might be the best thing she'd gotten from Bobby.

"I'm hungry." When had Bopper climbed down, and how had he sneaked up without Karen's noticing? "Can we get hamburgers?"

She nearly said yes out of habit. But they ate too much greasy food, and besides Karen didn't like frittering away money on junk.

"Chinese noodle soup," she said. "I'll make beef flavor, the one you like."

Bopper complained, but not much. He liked the packaged dried soup mix almost as much as a burger. The only thing it lacked was a free toy.

Terry bit his lip when he heard the menu, but he put on a brave front. "Yummy! My favorite!"

"You're a good sport," Karen whispered as the children ran toward the car. She hadn't expected him to act so cheerful about the prospect of soup for lunch.

"You hit me at a good time," he said. "I won the sword fight."

She laughed.

It was the kind of morning she hadn't had enough of, these past two years. A series of little moments that Karen wished she could frame and keep forever. Rose earnestly clucking to the llama to turn its head just so for a picture. Bopper scrambling to climb a fence in his eagerness to pet a pony, and Terry lifting him so he could reach.

In the rush to earn a living and tend to the hundreds of small demands that made up each day, it was easy to lose track of the thread of their lives. The children wouldn't be small forever. They wouldn't always center their activities around their mother, either. She'd heard enough moaning from friends who had teenagers to know she ought to enjoy this stage.

As they climbed into the car, Terry was humming. Karen shot him a questioning look. "A penny for your thoughts."

"I feel like I'm getting a second chance to be a kid," he said. "I guess this is what it means to be a parent, experiencing it over again."

From the corner of her eye, Karen saw Bopper's little frame stiffen in the backseat. He'd obviously overheard their conversation and didn't like it.

Terry caught her glance and swiveled. "What's the frown for?"

Bopper's lip quivered. "You're not my parent! I've already got a daddy! I'm not playing with you ever again!"

A flash of hurt darkened Terry's eyes, but his voice remained steady. "I didn't mean that I could take your daddy's place."

"You sure can't!" Bopper folded his arms and stared out the window.

"He's a different daddy," Rose advised her brother. "Like Anne of Green Gables lost her parents, but she got Marilla and Matthew."

"I'm not an orphan." He refused to look at her.

Terry gave Karen an apologetic shrug. "I didn't mean to make trouble."

"You didn't." This was a battle that had to be won by inches. "Bopper needs to come to terms with the situation in his own way."

"He won't," Rose predicted. "He's stubborn."

KAREN'S THIRTIETH birthday fell at the end of February. "Fell" seemed like the appropriate word that Sunday morning, as she lay in bed wondering how the years had managed to sneak by so quickly.

Her gaze traveled around the room. It hadn't changed much since Bobby left. The queen-size bed still bore the handmade quilt she'd found in an antique shop, the patchwork motif echoed in printed curtains. Her silver-backed mirror and brush sat on a doily atop the mahogany dresser. Above it, a mirror reflected Karen's own face back to her.

She didn't think she looked thirty, but what did thirty look like, anyway?

Not that she'd wasted her youth. An unbidden mental calculation totted up Karen's accomplishments: two children, a career, enough money from the sale of the house to give them a small nest egg.

Added to the modest inheritance from her grand-mother, it would at least ensure that her children could attend college.

Mental balance sheet aside, however, several things were missing from the equation. A sense that her work meant something to her, for one. And—Karen decided to be brutally frank—even though she could manage her life without a man, she missed the intimacy and emotional support she saw in her brother's marriage.

She'd never enjoyed that kind of closeness with Bobby. In retrospect, she could link her once frequent bouts of self-doubt to his snide comments on her lack of aesthetics. There'd been days when he refused to speak, leaving her feeling confused and guilty.

Damn Bobby! Well, she wasn't going to think about him today. As a matter of fact, since Terry moved in, Karen realized, she hadn't thought about her ex-husband nearly as much as she used to.

She sat up, listening for the children. She wished Bopper would bounce around upstairs like he usually did, knocking over toys as he burrowed through his closet and dragged out his train set or his miniature space station. These days he hardly played at all.

Time, the great healer. If only there were some way to juice it up a little!

She slid out of bed, grabbed some jeans and a T-shirt and tiptoed across the hall to the bathroom. Terry's door stood ajar, and Karen heard his deep, regular breathing. She envied his ability to sleep late.

A spray of hot water chased off the last traces of sluggishness. Her mother had promised to take her to lunch, and Karen had a lot to do before then.

Emerging a half hour later, she was surprised to smell something suspiciously like pancakes. Surely Rose wasn't cooking them unsupervised!

Downstairs, she found Terry demonstrating how to flip flapjacks. "It's all in the wrist," he told Rose. His hand jerked as Karen walked in, and the pancake landed with a splat! on top of the refrigerator.

"I think I could do that," Bopper said. They all laughed.

Spotting Karen, the children clustered around with their presents. Bopper presented her with a lopsided crayon drawing of a house, complete with stairs, an indoor swimming pool and a monster.

"That's amazing," she said and meant it.

Rose had tackled her project at school: a handmade book, stapled together, in which she'd copied and illustrated her favorite poems. "This is beautiful," Karen told her. "I couldn't have asked for better gifts."

"Then I guess I can keep mine," Terry teased.

"You're the landlord," she reminded him. "You don't need to give me anything, just keep the plumbing in order."

"I couldn't resist." He handed her a small white box.

"What is it? What is it?" Bopper demanded.

Karen would have preferred to open it alone, in case the contents turned out to be personal, but she didn't feel up to an extended debate with her son.

Inside the box, on a bed of cotton, nestled an enamel pin worked with three flowers: a rose, a pansy and an aster. It looked like a tiny garden, so perfectly wrought that Karen could almost smell the nectar.

"It's perfect," she said.

"It reminded me of you." Terry ran a hand through his hair. "The rose, of course, for your daughter, and the pansy because they look so delicate but stand up to the cold, and the aster, well, it's like a star. Something to aim for."

From the flush on his cheeks, he'd probably never expected to say anything so poetic. Karen wanted to kiss away his embarrassment, but she settled for ruffling his hair.

"I'll wear it today." She tucked the pin into her pocket for later.

"Mom." Rose turned from clearing the table. "Can I have lunch with you and Grandma?"

"You don't want to go to the mall with Bopper and me?" Terry asked.

"And do what?"

"Play video games. Eat pizza. And there's a special photography show."

Rose weighed her options. "What kind of photography?"

"All kinds. Bring your camera and take your own shots at the mall."

That was enough to persuade Rose. "Okay, I'll come."

With Terry's help, the morning's laundry was dispatched in record time. At eleven-thirty, Karen went upstairs with a luxurious half-hour break to change.

She slipped into a soft turquoise dress and fixed her hair and makeup. Staring into the mirror, she decided something was missing. Something round and enameled and cleverly wrought.

Pinning the enamel flowers in place, she traced the aster with her fingertip.

A star to aim for. Terry hadn't forgotten about her dream.

It was too late to sign up for classes this semester, but some community colleges in the area operated on the quarter system, and they'd be starting soon. Did she dare take him up on his offer to help?

Karen chided herself for her indecision. Thirty years old. She couldn't keep putting off her plans, telling herself there was plenty of time.

She'd get a current catalog first thing Monday and call every baby-sitter she knew. Surely some teenager would appreciate a standing once-a-week assignment and the regular pay that came with it.

The doorbell jerked Karen out of her reverie and she scrambled about in the closet for her shoes.

As she came down the stairs she saw that Rose had already answered the door. Her mother's tall figure bent to hug the eager young girl, their entwined figures bathed in a halo of light.

Helene's face glowed as she embraced her granddaughter. A sweet peacefulness supplanted Rose's usual worried expression.

Always Karen had been the link between grandmother and granddaughter. Now, seeing the love that flowed between them, she felt as if she'd witnessed the handing down of an invisible torch.

They separated, both glowing. Helene caught sight of Karen. "Happy birthday!"

"Where's Sid?" Karen's brother had planned to bring their mother on his way back from a delivery.

"I drove myself," Helene said.

"You what?"

"I've been taking driving lessons. Don't worry. I've got my license." Her mother grinned like the Cheshire cat. "Surprised?"

"I certainly am," Karen said.

Bopper came to hug his grandmother, too, and then they emerged to find an aging Mercedes in the driveway. "My first car." Helene regarded it with pride.

"What brought this on?" Without thinking, Karen walked toward the driver's door.

"You're sitting on that side." Helene pointed. "Don't worry. It's safe."

Karen smothered her nervousness. "Of course it is."

When they were both belted in, her mother backed smoothly out of the driveway. "Where would you like to eat?"

"I'm not sure." Most of her old favorites had closed over the years and Karen rarely had time to dine out these days, unless you counted burger joints. "Why don't we just cruise uptown Whittier?"

"Good idea." Helene nodded. "It's changed so much, I hardly know it."

You've changed, too, Karen added mentally. Was it Frederick who had motivated her to learn to drive? After so many years...

Well, why not? Karen discovered she was actually taking pride in her mother's newfound expertise as they drove through the side streets toward Greenleaf Avenue.

She soon forgot even to notice her mother's driving technique and fell to studying the houses as they passed. Being free to watch the landscape was a rare treat.

Karen noticed a new unpainted porch and foundation attached to an old house, a reminder of the 1987 Whittier Narrows earthquake. Most of the fallen or damaged buildings had been torn down or rebuilt by now, but a few were still undergoing reconstruction.

Whittier was that anomaly, a relatively old—or at least not-so-new—city in Southern California. Originating as a Quaker colony in 1887, it had been named for the poet John Greenleaf Whittier, although he'd been too frail to visit his namesake.

More than a hundred years later, Whittier managed to maintain a nineteenth-century small-town quality in the midst of a late-twentieth-century building boom. The tree-lined uptown area felt both picturesque and eclectic, with its mix of Victorian, Spanish and neo-Colonial architecture. Stores featured antiques, jewelry, clothes, art supplies and books, while cracked sidewalks opened into newly installed mosaic-like whorls of red brick.

Karen supposed the updating might look hodge-podge, but she respected the city leaders for choosing not to raze and rebuild everything. Cities should reflect the changing eras through which they had grown, she felt.

"Oh!" Helene's intake of breath was scarcely audible, but it alerted Karen.

She followed her mother's gaze to a shiny 1950s-style restaurant called the Rocky Cola Café that dominated one corner.

"Let's stop here," Karen said.

"Well . . . all right." Her mother sounded pleased.

They angled into a parking slot along the street. Helene killed the motor and sat silent for a moment.

"Remind you of something?" Karen prodded.

"The restaurant?" Helene blinked as she slowly returned from her thoughts. "Well, it did put me in mind of the fifties. Of your father and . . . things."

"Being young?" Karen guessed. As she grew up, she'd never thought about her mother's youth, assuming, like most kids, that Mom had been born in the role of mother. The way Rose and Bopper probably thought about her.

"It's not so much that it brings back the past," Helene murmured. "It's more that, well, the architecture seems so natural. As if we'd gone back to reality."

"Reality, here we come," Karen teased.

They walked into the restaurant, pleased to find it wasn't crowded.

"I'll bet fifties cafés never really looked like this." Neon-veined paintings flashed on the walls and tubes of flowing purple, green and melon arched over the jukebox.

"None of the ones I went to," Helene admitted as a hostess led them across the red-and-white checkered floor to a red booth. From here, they commanded an excellent view of the Coca-Cola sign painted on one wall.

"I suppose it does feel as if we should be able to go back and visit the past." Karen opened her menu. "As if it should all still be there, waiting."

"I wish my children and grandchildren could know the world I grew up in," Helene admitted. "Rose and Bopper can't imagine life without videos and computers. And you can't imagine it without television and rock music."

"Thanks, Mom." Karen grinned at her. "I don't feel so old any more."

They took their time reading the menu. After they ordered, Helene folded her hands on the table. She started to speak, then bit her lip.

"Mom," Karen said. "Are you nervous about something?"

Helene nodded.

"You didn't just suggest having lunch together because it's my birthday, did you?" Karen guessed. "Out with it."

"Frederick and I are getting married."

The statement hung in midair. Bold, decisive and final. In Karen's mind, it took on a life of its own.

Her mother, her sweet, helpless mother, had learned to drive so she could come to Karen with what could only be considered a declaration of independence. Not that a woman in her fifties needed anyone's permission to get married.

Karen wasn't sure why she felt so taken aback. Frederick seemed like a charming gentleman. He would give her mother much happiness.

Yet as long as Karen could remember, she—and, as he got older, Sid—had been taking care of Helene. They'd cleaned out father's belongings after he died, invested their mother's money, even helped find her a condominium when she moved back to West Los Angeles.

Somewhere along the line, Karen realized, she'd lost touch with Helene's thoughts and day-to-day activities. Part of her life had slipped into the past without her realizing it. The mother she'd taken for granted had metamorphosed into a dynamic stranger.

"Aren't you pleased?" Helene's forehead creased anxiously.

"Oh, Mom!" Karen took her mother's hand. "Of course I am! I was just sitting here thinking that, well, that you've changed."

"Blame Frederick." Helene's eyes sparkled. "I don't know how he does it. He manages to take care of me and prod me at the same time. He simply expects me to act like a competent adult. I realized I couldn't expect him to baby me, and I should never have expected it of you and Sid.''

''You didn't—''

''I did,'' Helene said. ''And I'm embarrassed to admit it, but for a while I resented the fact that you were busy with your own lives. Oh, I knew I'd chosen to move away, to be back with my old friends. And it was my own fault I'd never learned to drive. But I felt like you owed me more attention.''

''You never told us!'' Karen stared at her, aghast.

''Because it was unreasonable of me.'' Helene sighed. ''And I didn't want to antagonize you. So for a while I wore my self-pity around like a widow's veil. Until I ran into Frederick again, and we started going out. I wanted him to respect me, and I realized I didn't respect myself.''

Karen bit back a response as the waitress appeared with their food. Once the woman had left, she said, ''We enjoyed helping you.''

''Not long-distance you didn't.'' Helene shook her head. ''Maybe I was testing you by moving away. Wanting you both to prove how much I mattered. But how could I, when you had small children to take care of? When Bobby left, that snapped me out of it. A few months later I saw Frederick at a party and I realized it was a sign, that I simply had to change.''

''Let me help plan the wedding,'' Karen said. ''When is it?''

''In three weeks.'' Helene pulled an invitation from her purse. ''It's all arranged. We're going to have it in the clubhouse at my condo complex.''

''But . . . our church . . .''

"I'm too old for all that formality." Helene waved a hand. "We thought of eloping, but Frederick felt that was carrying things too far."

As they discussed the wedding, Karen's head spun. Her mother's newfound independence marked the end of a chapter in her life. It reminded her that there would be other chapters, other endings and beginnings, that the circumstances she thought of as reality were only temporary.

Someday Rose and Bopper, too, would take their lives in their hands. They'd plunge into the world and set their own courses. Which was how it ought to be.

Thinking about it made Karen feel dizzy.

As their dishes were cleared for dessert, Helene noticed Karen's pin. "Birthday present?"

She touched it. "From Terry."

"He seems like a good man."

"I'm sure Marian's kept you informed," Karen teased.

"She says you're moving out this summer." Helene drew herself up as the waitress presented her with a hot apple dumpling. "My, that looks good.... Well, you're a damn fool if you do."

"Mom!"

"Take a chance, Karen," said her mother. "It's time you learned to trust again."

"I'm not sure Terry wants to be trusted," Karen said. "Not with too much responsibility."

"Sometimes you have to take a chance," Helene said. "Let yourself lean on somebody. You've always been the one to take care of others. It's time you accepted a little help."

"I have!" she said, adding, "From Sid and Marian."

"That's different. They're relatives."

"I'll think about it." Karen didn't want to argue, but her instincts warned her to take this relationship slowly, slowly, slowly. She couldn't chance another catastrophe like Bobby.

Although she'd enjoyed lunching with her mother, Karen couldn't deny a twinge of relief when she found herself on her front walkway again, waving goodbye as Helene drove off. She needed the comfort of her familiar routines to check the sense that events were leaping beyond control.

She looked up at the old, familiar house. How she loved this place, even though she no longer owned it. It stood as it had for nearly a century, ready to shelter her family from the unexpected gusts of fate.

Except...

Why was Terry's car still parked in the driveway? Surely he and the kids hadn't returned from the mall already....

Across the street sat a van that she'd hardly noticed when she and Helene pulled up. Karen turned to inspect it with a rising sense of dread.

The same battered blue paint. The same dented fender.

Why did it have to be today, on her birthday?

Stiffly she let herself in the front door. She didn't think she'd made any noise at all, but instantly a familiar stocky figure materialized in the dining room doorway.

"Karen!" said Bobby. "Happy birthday!"

Chapter Ten

Bopper scurried out of the kitchen behind his father. "Daddy's here!" His little face glowed with joy.

A voice inside warned Karen to tread gently. She knew her ex-husband to be a self-centered jerk, but she couldn't expect a five-year-old to see that.

If she forced Bobby to leave, she would become the villain in Bopper's eyes. So she took a deep breath and said, "How nice of you to come wish me happy birthday."

"Uh...I didn't.... Yeah!" How like Bobby not even to have remembered her birthday.

He looked bloated and much older. Although he'd barely reached his thirties, Bobby's hair was thinning around the temples and his lack of muscle tone testified to too much beer and too little exercise.

A wave of relief washed through her when Terry appeared from the kitchen, one arm around Rose's waist. The little girl's lips pinched together as she stared at her father. Bobby, as usual, ignored her to concentrate on Bopper.

"My little man!" he declared. "Can you believe this? He's grown six inches!"

"That tends to happen." Karen couldn't keep the bite out of her voice. "When you don't see your son for two years."

"Hey, hey, let's not argue!" Bobby failed to meet her eyes. "Guys! I've got presents in the car!"

Bopper ran outside with his father. Terry gave Karen a helpless shrug.

"He apparently still has a key," he explained. "We started for the mall, then came back to get my wallet, and here he was."

"Bopper's been drooling all over him." Rose looked as if she might burst into tears.

"He hasn't been cuddling his little girl, has he?" Karen hugged her daughter. "Oh, Rosie, it's not anything about you. Your Dad's just so wrapped up in himself, he doesn't see anybody else."

"He sees Bopper," Rose said.

Terry rumpled her hair. "I've got a hunch he sees his son as an extension of himself. As if he could be young again and have all his chances back. But sooner or later—and I'm betting on sooner—he's going to realize that Bopper's a separate person."

"Then he'll leave." Karen tried her best to rein in the anger. "And we'll have to do our best to pick up the pieces."

Rose looked at Terry. "I'm glad you're here." She headed for the stairs. "I'll be in my room. I don't want his presents." She took the steps two at a time.

Terry stared after her. "Her attitude bothers me more than Bopper's. She's holding so much inside."

"I despise that man!" Karen quivered with fury. "But I know better than to show it. Bopper's got to see the truth for himself. Or as much of it as a five-year-old can handle."

"Maybe Bobby will surprise us. Maybe he's changed." Terry didn't sound very hopeful.

Bobby returned, and soon they were sitting at a dining-room table piled with torn shopping bags and battered boxes. The presents turned out to be Bobby's artwork from the past two years.

He'd tried his hand at pottery and ended up with a series of lumps splattered with patchy glazes and bequeathed high-flown titles like "The Theater Personified" and "The Independence of the Spirit."

Bopper loved them. "Wow! These are just like rocks!" He lined up a series of ceramic clots in descending order of size. "This is the daddy rock, and here's the mommy and these are the babies."

Next Bobby produced tie-dyed and batiked fabric that looked as if it had been created by a strung-out hippie in the sixties. Like an overenthusiastic child, he'd thrown in every color on the palette, but instead of a rainbow he'd come up with a mess.

"These are great!" Bopper wrapped a strip of olive green, turquoise and yellow fabric around his head. "I'm a Ninja Turtle! Michelangelo!"

"Uh, yeah." His father glared disapprovingly, fingers quivering as if itching to snatch the cloth away. Then he caught sight of Karen's narrowed eyes and turned his attention to the remaining "gifts."

Bobby's latest work proved to be miniature "portraits" tucked into dime store frames. The tiny canvases gave an impression of cuteness because they were so small, but that was all that could be said for them.

A child might have done them, and not a talented child, either. Splotchy eyes dripped into cartoon noses, colors had muddied. There was no focus, no style, just dabs of paint.

"I'm getting back into collages," Bobby assured them. "Now that I've extended my range."

"That's . . . quite a collection," Terry said.

"Where'd you put the hammer, Karen?" Bobby glanced around as if carpentry tools ought to be lying on the sideboard. "I thought I'd hang a few things."

"You what? Bobby . . ."

Before she could finish, Terry said, "You know, Bobby, the house belongs to me now. Karen's just renting."

"So?" Bobby rewrapped the ceramic lumps, in spite of the fact that Bopper had been playing with them.

"So maybe I need to think about how I want to display any new artwork," Terry said diplomatically.

"Yeah, sure, whatever." Bobby had never been good at confrontations. Karen also wasn't sure he really grasped the fact that she'd had to give up the house because he didn't pay any support. "What's for dinner?"

"Since it's Karen's birthday, I thought we might order out." Terry shot him a look on the keen edge of exasperation.

"Yeah, fine." Bobby leaned back in his chair and thumped his dirty jogging shoes onto the table. "It sure feels good to be home. You wouldn't believe those slobs at the art colony."

"Daddy, you're not supposed to put your shoes on the table," Bopper warned.

Bobby didn't seem to hear. "You wouldn't believe how lazy they are."

"I think I might," Karen couldn't resist saying.

"They're all convinced they're the next Picasso." Bobby tilted the chair at a dangerous angle. "They wouldn't know real talent if it came up and bit them."

Bopper tried to tilt his chair back like his father's and would have tipped over if Terry hadn't grabbed him.

Bobby went on. "I don't belong there."

"Are you trying to tell me you've left them for—" Karen let the words trail off. The thought was too horrible to speak aloud.

"I'm back!" Bobby grinned. "Ain't that great?"

"You seem to have overlooked a few things," Karen began, until she noticed her son's features tightening with anger. Let Bobby dig his own grave. "We'll have to see," she finished.

"This place is looking up." Bobby straightened. "Those guinea pigs in the laundry room! Great touch."

"Chinchillas," Terry murmured.

"And I love the rowing machine in the spare bedroom!" Bobby waved his arms. "This house could turn into a work of environmental art! We could dig out the Christmas lights and those pink-glass globes..."

"You broke them." Rose's voice pierced the air from the landing. "You broke my ornaments, Daddy."

"I'll bet your Mom got you some better ones!" He jumped up. "Listen, Rosie, Bobby Junior. Wanna turn this place into a space station? I mean, a whole space environment? That rowing machine gives me an idea!"

Bopper hopped to his feet, knocking his chair over. "Yeah, yeah!" He raced up the stairs after his father.

Rose looked intrigued, in spite of herself. "Mom?"

Give him enough rope to hang himself. "It's okay," Karen said. "Really, Rose."

Every instinct screamed for her to rush upstairs and supervise the goings-on. To protect her children from this spoiled brat of a father. But she knew he wouldn't actually harm them.

"You're amazing." Terry straightened Bopper's overturned chair. "In your place, I'd have popped him one."

"Half of me hopes they have a great time," Karen admitted. "The other half hopes he screws up royally."

"It'll probably be a little of both." Terry steered her into the living room.

She kept one ear cocked for noises from upstairs. Occasionally she heard excited voices and thumps on the steps leading to Bopper's tower.

Terry shook his head. "A herd of elephants up there."

"What if he really stays?" Karen realized, as she asked the question, that she was relying on Terry's support to deal with whatever might come.

"He'll have to find his own place." Terry's calm certainty reassured her. "First of all, I couldn't stand to have him living here. And second, he is your *ex*-husband. You may have to share the children, but you don't have to take care of him."

"Old habits," Karen admitted.

"Don't worry." Terry stretched and got up from the table. "We can handle him, Karen."

She loved the "we."

They were reading the morning newspaper, stretched companionably at opposite ends of the sofa with their legs brushing, when the first indications of dissent drifted downstairs.

Karen didn't enjoy the stage whispers wafting from upstairs—"He won't like that...!" "He won't have to know...."—followed by a heavy creak. Terry didn't respond, even though he must realize his rowing machine was being moved.

"Could they damage it?" she asked.

"Not likely." Terry turned a page. "I think we should stay out of this as long as possible."

Karen knew he was right, but she couldn't concentrate on the front page. Terry distracted her by reading the comics aloud.

"Daddy, no!" came Bopper's cry a few minutes later. "You broke my spaceship!"

"It's just Legos." Karen knew Bobby well enough to picture him just barreling ahead. "I need them for my tracking station."

"They're mine!" That was the way Bopper yelled when he'd been pushed too far.

Karen set the newspaper aside. "I'd better go up."

Terry waved her back. "Let me try. You don't want to get caught in the middle."

"I don't want Bopper blaming you, either," she said.

"Bobby and I don't have any old tapes between us." He swiveled into a sitting position. "Maybe we can keep this thing civilized."

"Thanks, Terry. More than you know."

He shot her a V-for-Victory sign and went upstairs.

TERRY STOOD AT THE head of the steps, taking in the second-floor hallway.

His rowing machine had been dragged into the doorway of his room, where it had stuck. Moving in, he and Mitch had had to angle it sharply to get through, so he wasn't surprised Bobby couldn't extract it by himself. Wouldn't it have been nice, though, if Bobby had put the exerciser back in place?

The rest of the hallway was strewn with pillows, a chair elevated shakily on blocks, Terry's white Christmas lights taped to the walls and trailing up to the third floor, and, hanging upside-down from the ceiling, an assortment of old dolls and plastic toy parts.

Rose's door was shut tight.

Terry supposed that if you tilted your head and squinted, you could sort of visualize the hallway as the bridge of a star cruiser and the dangling objects as indications of zero gravity.

"You're ruining it!" Bopper screamed from the tower. "Stop it, Daddy!"

"Hey, calm down. This is a great tracking station."

The sound of a foot stomping made it clear that Bopper wasn't impressed.

Terry mounted to the tower, his footsteps dragging. He hated emotional blowups. He preferred making a joke and distracting people to dealing with difficult issues head-on.

But it was too late to escape.

"Hi." Terry poked his head into Bopper's room. Or what used to be Bopper's room. It was mostly a mess right now: books heaped on the floor, the mattress half off the bed, Legos stuck together every which way atop the bureau and box springs.

"How do you like our Martian landscape?" Bobby crowed. "Listen, you got a camera? I need to capture it on film."

"Gee, I haven't seen my camera since I moved," Terry said.

"I've got one." How Rose had managed to follow him unnoticed he wasn't sure, but he *had* been lost in thought. The little girl held up the box camera she'd employed so gleefully in the park. "I'll take your pictures, Daddy."

That was one of the things he loved about the kid, that she'd give even the most self-centered parent a second chance. Terry wanted to hug her.

Bobby waved the offer aside. "I'm talking about a real camera. Terry, go see if you can find it, will you?"

Rose fled. Bopper stuck his lip out and began jumping as hard as he could all over the box springs and the mattress. Terry tensed, ready to grab the boy if he fell.

"Cut it out!" Bobby deposited his son on the floor.

"Bopper, come help me find my camera." Then Terry remembered that the entrance to his room was blocked. "Bobby, you need to move the rowing machine so I can get in."

"I'm sure we can climb over." Bobby shrugged. "Oh, all right."

With Terry doing most of the work, they wrestled the rowing machine out of the way. When they found the camera tucked in a drawer, Terry loaded some film and turned it over to Bobby.

Upstairs, the would-be artist climbed around, shooting pictures upside down and at odd angles. Terry studied him, trying to visualize how he had looked ten years ago. That thinning hair must have been a shock of reddish curls like Bopper's, and a remaining trace of freckles hinted at a youthful profusion.

Years of frustration must have turned boyish petulance into the unappealing churlishness Terry had already glimpsed. He felt a twinge of sympathy, remembering the pain when his first novel fluttered home in a sheaf of rejection slips. He felt grateful that, unlike Bobby, he'd been able to achieve the goals he set for himself. It must be hard to have such a giant ego and such an apparent lack of ability.

Then Terry thought about the tears in Rose's eyes and his sympathy disappeared.

Bobby finished the roll on the second-floor landing. "Yeah, great. Which room is mine?'

Terry met Bopper's eye's and nodded slightly toward the tower. He was glad when the boy caught his drift and vanished upstairs.

"Listen," Terry said. "There's a little problem."

"It's okay." Bobby pocketed the film. "I can sleep on the couch."

Terry decided to try tact. He'd always wanted to develop some, and what better time than now? "This isn't the best environment for an artist, is it?" he said. "You know how demanding kids can be."

"They're at school all day, right?" Bobby fiddled with a strand of lights that had pulled loose.

Terry shuddered at the thought of trying to work in the same house with this overgrown preschooler. "And you know, Karen and the kids are moving next month." It wasn't really that soon, but why put a fine point on it? "Karen's got her eye on a duplex, a two-bedroom."

Bobby grimaced. "Oh." Then he brightened "You won't need this whole place to yourself, right?"

It was on the tip of Terry's tongue to make up some lie about friends moving in, but he didn't like lying. He didn't like this whole conversation.

"Forget it," he said. "I bought this house. I decide who moves in. And who moves the furniture, and what gets stuck up on the walls. You haven't asked my permission once today, for anything, Bobby. Karen had to sell this house because she couldn't afford to keep it. She's been a good sport about it. I don't have to be a good sport. I wasn't married to you, and I'm not the mother of your children.''

Bobby shifted uncomfortably. "But I'm giving you all this free, you know? The artwork. Like, you'd have to pay thousands of dollars for something like this."

"I doubt it."

Terry wasn't sure where his voice had gotten the steely edge. He discovered he enjoyed the sense of taking control.

"You know, I got lots of places to go," Bobby grumbled. "I mean, three, four people used to live at the art colony invited me to come stay with them. Places like New Mexico and Montana. Where you got real people and clean air."

"Sounds terrific," Terry said.

"So maybe in a few days I'll be moving on."

Terry resisted the urge to drag Bobby out of the house this very minute. "You can start by cleaning up."

"You mean tear up my own work?" The freckles quivered.

"I mean take down the mess you've made in *my* house." Terry kept his tone even.

"I got some old pals in Pasadena." Bobby edged toward the stairs. "They're, you know, expecting me."

"Don't forget to take the stuff on the dining-room table." Terry couldn't bring himself to characterize it as art.

"Yeah, yeah."

"Aren't you forgetting something?"

Bobby noticed the camera in his hand. "Oh. Here." He handed it back without so much as a thank you. "I'd like to say goodbye to the kids but I think they're kind of angry. I guess I don't exactly blame them. Tell them I'll miss them, okay?"

"I wish you could tell them yourself," Terry said, but Bobby didn't seem to hear as he hurried downstairs.

KAREN STOPPED OUTSIDE the bathroom. Standing there in her robe, her mouth tingling from a thorough brushing, she reveled in the silence.

The only light came from downstairs, where she could hear Terry in the kitchen, cleaning up the remains of her birthday cupcakes. Two batches, chocolate *and* lemon. They'd really overdone it, but she didn't care.

Today, she felt, they'd all turned a corner. Bopper and Rose had withdrawn into themselves for a while after Bobby left. Karen, cleaning up the junk strewn in the hall, had wondered how best to run damage control.

Effortlessly Terry had done it for her. He'd gone upstairs to Bopper's room and helped the little boy build his own version of a space station, one that was fun for a five-year-old.

Then he'd pretended Rose was a famous actress celebrating her own thirtieth birthday. Naturally she'd needed dress-up clothes and shoes and had made a raid on Karen's closet, but who cared? Her little girl was smiling again.

They'd dined on pizza and cupcakes. It was the best birthday Karen could remember.

She'd read somewhere that when a bone healed crooked, sometimes you had to break it again to set it right. That was kind of what had happened today, she supposed as she went into the bedroom and began hanging up the clothes Rose had left.

Seeing Bobby had taken the lid off a cauldron of unresolved emotions—resentment, regret, guilt. For Bopper and Rose, it had provided one last chance to test their hope that Daddy might live up to their expectations.

Crash and burn. Painful as it had proved, she couldn't help but believe that her children were now on the road to recovery. There would always be some hurt connected with their father's inadequacies, but at least they wouldn't torture themselves with might-have-beens.

Karen sat on the edge of the bed, a flower-print dress draped over one arm. She'd nearly got caught up again, letting Bobby ride roughshod over her. It was so hard to break out of old patterns. Unless you had the right kind of help.

Bobby had slunk downstairs after his confrontation with Terry. "Who needs that old crab?" he'd said. "Honey, let's move out of here. Get an apartment for the four of us. This is my home, too, you know."

For a split second, an echo of her old self had considered the possibility. In defiance of all logic, she'd wondered if it wouldn't be best for the children to live with both their parents.

"No," she'd heard herself say. "Bobby, I would never try to keep the children from seeing you, if they want to. But you're out of my life. You have to take responsibility for yourself now."

"I'm an *artist!*" he'd howled, gathering his self-respect around him like a tattered blanket. "I don't have to take responsibility!"

"Then live with the consequences," she'd said.

That was the hardest part. Cutting him loose. Watching his shoulders hunch as if to ward off a blow.

He'd thrust his pathetic miniatures and tie-dyed fabric into the sack and hugged it tight as he stalked out the door.

"Goodbye," she'd called. He hadn't answered.

The funny thing was that as she watched him stomp down the front walkway, he shrank. He didn't really get smaller—it was more that, as Karen watched, the man who had dominated a decade of her life became just a guy she used to know.

Goodbye, Bobby.

She looked up as Terry stepped into the room. He didn't usually come in here. Sharing a house this way, they'd tacitly agreed that each had to maintain privacy or they'd cross an invisible boundary that they could never retrace.

Tonight, Karen didn't mind. She realized that emotionally she'd felt before as if she were waiting for her divorce to become final. Now it had.

From the bed, Terry scooped up the satiny blue dress she'd worn on that long-ago night when they'd danced together downstairs. He held it up as if it were a woman, bowed his head in princely fashion and extended one arm, extending the sleeve as if the dress were his partner.

Terry hummed a few bars of "I Could Have Danced All Night" and whirled around the room with his invisible lady. It was a silly antic but he made it look charming.

He put the dress aside and quirked an eyebrow at Karen. She stood up, curtsied and glided into his arms. They waltzed, slower and slower, until they were simply standing with their arms around each other.

"Thank you," Karen said.

"I haven't done anything yet."

She started to laugh. His mouth closed over hers. Karen couldn't remember what had seemed so funny.

His kiss was intense, probing, as if he were trying to burrow into her. He gripped her arms, pulling her close.

The silver butterflies woven into the blue dress must have escaped, because they were clouding the room, turning the air to silver and steam. Silver in Terry's tongue and in her blood. Steam melting their bodies together, wrapping them inside a world of pulsating heat.

There was no time for words. She felt Terry lowering her onto the bed and tasting her skin, and she could no longer tell where he left off and she began.

A blue-white flood raged across Karen's skin, a torrent bursting through the dam.

She would have cried out, would have begged, but there was no need. The tide had caught Terry, too. They rolled together, discovering the tender flesh beneath each other's clothing, the sensitive curves and soft vulnerable inlets that made each of them moan.

The storm broke for a moment—he lifted his head and their eyes met in shared wonder—and then the force of a hurricane thrust him inside her.

Again and again they met, wild foam at the edge of the shore, the thunder of surf rising and falling and sweeping them into the depths. They lost their bearings in the mist and surfaced in the sunlit splendor of a tropical sea.

Terry claimed her by a brilliant coral reef, on an untamed beach, beneath an emerald waterfall. The current dashed them back into the ocean, across the white-tipped waves, riding a curl that surged and peaked and flung them both into a shower of steam.

Karen lay in a silver afterglow, wondering when the beach had turned back into a bed and whether the hurricane had shown up on any radar.

Several minutes passed before Terry stirred. "Are we still on Planet Earth?" She nodded. "I could have sworn..."

"If you're going to tell me you see little green men when you make love..."

"You'll what?" He pulled her against him. "Make me do it all over again?"

"Something like that," she murmured into his shoulder.

She was weighing the possibility of kissing him, when she dozed off. Sometime in the night Karen thought she heard Terry say, "If you still want to take that class, I'll watch the kids."

Chapter Eleven

The problem with Monday mornings was the quiet. Terry could hardly stand it.

He wandered through the empty house, missing the children, missing Karen and drinking his coffee. He'd made instant, and it had a harsh taste. Maybe he should brew a pot in the coffee maker.

On the other hand, maybe he ought to get his tail upstairs and start writing.

But not yet. Not until he'd rummaged through the refrigerator for a leftover cupcake, even though he was pretty sure they'd all been eaten. Not until he'd wiped a crumb off the table, then picked it off the floor, then wiped up the coffee he'd spilled in the process.

It was amazing how many things you could find to do when you were trying to get out of writing.

Terry set down the cup and went to feed the chinchillas. Gloompuss rattled around when she heard him. Phil rolled happily in a tray of gray dust, fluffing his fur. The babies licked droplets of water off the hanging bottle and watched Terry's approach.

He filled their bowl with pellets and debated whether to chop some fresh greens. He checked the refrigerator, discovered the vegetable bin was empty and seized joyously on the possibility of heading for the supermarket.

No, and no.

He forced himself up the stairs. Left foot, right foot. Left foot, right foot. Like a refugee from a Dr. Seuss book.

In his office, he took a moment to focus his thoughts. He pushed away memories of last night, of making love with Karen in the den after the children fell asleep. He tried to ignore the lingering impression of her gray eyes dark with longing.

Back to the Thing in the Closet. He still hadn't figured out where the story was going. Okay, some ancient evil had been brought to the New World by mistake and achieved symbiosis with nasty old Gladys Maycap. And so far it had eaten one aging burglar, a snooty social climber, one rude meter reader and a con artist who tried to pull the pigeon drop on the wrong pigeon. But why? What was its goal? What ultimate evil must Bridget Weintraub overcome in between selling venetian blinds?

The phone rang one and a half times. Terry grabbed it. "Terry, hello?" came the clipped voice of his agent, Howard Hallowsmith.

Some children might be born with silver spoons in their mouths—with Howard, it must have been a telephone. He sometimes carried on two or three phone conversations at one time.

"Thought I'd let you know," he began, and then called to someone in his office, "The pink copy!" To Terry, he said, "Italian rights. Four thousand."

"*Lire* or dollars?" Terry knew he had to keep his questions brief or they'd get lost.

"Dollars. They have your IRS forms?" Authors had to file a tax exemption with each country to which they sold foreign rights, or they'd end up paying taxes twice.

"Yes—"

"Okay." To someone else, "Tell her we're withholding dramatic rights. That's nonnegotiable!" To Terry, "Called Joe Lancer. Promises, promises."

The producer hadn't paid for his extension yet. But Terry wasn't eager to reclaim the rights—no one else had expressed interest. And the way Joe was hustling, surely he'd have a movie package put together within a few months.

"I know you're doing your best," he told the agent.

"Okay, let's see," muttered Howard. "*Ghoul of the Golden West.* Pushed back the publication date."

"I know. Any word about promotion? A publicist?"

"Not yet," Howard said. "How's the new house?"

"Great . . ." Terry made the mistake of pausing for a breath.

"Terrific! Catch you later!" Click.

Terry dropped the phone into its cradle and mentally ran through what Howard had said. Four thousand dollars, minus ten percent, would be winging its way to him in the next few months. That was the good news.

The rest made him squirm. He hadn't expected the movie deal to take this long to come together. The way Joe Lancer talked, every big-name director in Hollywood had expressed keen interest at one time or other. And the new novel—if the publisher was so excited about it, why hadn't a publicist been assigned?

Terry didn't like worrying about money. Brooding went against his nature.

Under normal circumstances, he wouldn't have given the matter much thought. The worst that could happen was that he'd have to sell the house. It would probably mean losing money, but financial security had never been one of his priorities.

Only now he had to think about Karen. He hadn't meant to lie to her—it had seemed innocent enough, letting her think he'd paid for the house outright. If he had to sell it now, he'd look like even more of a louse than Bobby.

"WHY DO YOU HAVE TO drive all the way to Saddleback College?" Rose asked over dinner that night.

Karen refilled Bopper's glass of water. "Because the local campus is on the semester system and it's too late for me to enroll. Saddleback's on the quarter system."

"Quarter of what?" The vagaries of class schedules were a bit complicated for a seven year old.

"Don't worry," Karen said. "I know it's an hour drive, but you'll be here with Terry."

She glanced at him. He was tucking into his linguine primavera with the same distracted air he'd worn all day. Karen wondered if he was having second thoughts about the promise he'd made.

She wanted to touch his cheek, to smooth his rumpled hair and brush his mouth with hers. She missed the freedom to play the natural role of new lovers, lost in each other. To slide into his lap and kiss him, to forget about dinner and schedules.

Bopper slopped water onto the table. Karen wiped it with her napkin. "Terry?" she asked.

"Mmmph?" He looked up with the startled expression of a student caught daydreaming in class.

"You still want to baby-sit?" Karen tried to sound nonchalant. Taking a class meant a lot to her. Even more, she needed to feel that Terry was willing to take some responsibility for her family. But she wouldn't force him.

All day, whenever she had time for a spare thought at work, she'd battled the impulse to make plans. To assume that because they were lovers, she and Terry had a future together.

Only if I can be sure he won't turn into another Bobby.

"Baby-sitting?" she prompted.

"Of course." He reached for the fruit salad and ladled some onto his plate. "This pasta is great. You're a fantastic cook."

"It's nutritious, too," Rose said. Her class had been studying the links between diet and health. "See? There's no cholesterol and hardly any fat."

Terry stared down at his plate in dismay. "I think I'm having a Big Mac Attack."

"I had a nice chat with the secretary in the business department today," Karen went on. "There's a class in office management that sounds like just what I need. It'll update me on information processing, as well as teach me about organizing and staffing."

"Sounds... efficient." Terry helped himself to seconds of linguine. "The broccoli has a terrific flavor."

"It's from the garlic," Rose said.

"I thought so." Terry nodded.

"It starts this Thursday," Karen said. "That's not too soon, is it?"

"No, of course—" His fork halfway to his mouth, Terry paused. "Thursdays?"

Karen stared at him. "That's your critique group night, isn't it? Oh, Terry, it's the only night the class is offered! But..."

He set down his fork. "It's okay. I'll work it out."

"I couldn't—" Couldn't what? Couldn't ask him to make a sacrifice? The alternative was for her to make a sacrifice instead.

"I promised to watch the kids and I will." If Terry's voice sounded vaguely strangled, Karen couldn't blame him. Neither of them had counted on this complication.

"We'll help you, Terry," Rose said. "You read me your book and I'll tell you what I think."

"Me, too!" Bopper piped up.

"Good deal." He smiled. Under the table, his knee bumped Karen's. It might have been an accident, but it sent quivers up her leg. Another hour until the kids' bedtime and then...

A loud crash from the front porch shot Karen to her feet. "What the—"

"I'll go." Terry waved her back. "You guys stay here."

Bopper's eyes got big. "What is it?"

"Lions and tigers," teased Karen, although she couldn't help feeling apprehensive. That crash had sounded like someone dropping a load of scrap metal. She had visions of a drunken driver ploughing his car into the front door.

"Hello?" she heard Terry say, and then, "Fantastic! I always wanted one of these!"

That was all it took to inspire a headlong rush from the table, Bopper scampering ahead of Rose.

"I'm just getting the hang of it." Peering outside, Karen recognized Lou Loomis, Terry's old friend from the ad agency. He was sitting in the middle of a contraption that took up the entire front porch.

Karen identified a pair of cymbals, a harmonica held aloft by a metal rod, drums and a small keyboard.

"It's a one-man band," Lou explained. "What I've always wanted. I got it at a garage sale."

Before she could respond, the air filled with clanging, tinkling, wheezing and thumping that must have shaken the neighbors from their dinner tables.

"I don't think—" she began.

"Wait! Wait!" Terry raced past her into the house.

"Can I play?" Bopper tried to climb up beside Lou. "What's that? How does this work? Does it have batteries?"

In a flash Terry had returned, carrying an assortment of children's musical instruments that had accumulated in the den over the years: a recorder flute, a tambourine, a guitar and a trumpet.

"Oh, no." Karen stared toward the street in horror. "Look, let's move this indoors, okay?"

"It won't fit," Lou pointed out, reasonably. "I've been practicing all weekend. I needed an audience and you were the first people I thought of."

"Let's get this show on the road." Terry distributed the trumpet to Bopper, the recorder to Rose and the tambourine to Karen. On the guitar, he strummed the opening chords of "When the Saints Go Marching In."

"All right!" cried Lou, joining in with a crash, a rat-a-tat-tat and a glissando.

The children squeaked and honked, off-key and off the rhythm. Karen stared around helplessly.

Mr. and Mrs. Rivers from next door were the first to peer out. Then the thirteen-year-old twins came bounding from across the street, followed by an elderly couple who lived two houses down and whom Karen had only met briefly on Christmas Eve, when they'd admired Terry's electric light display.

She tensed, awaiting the first angry words. Instead, Mr. and Mrs. Rivers emerged with a clarinet and a trumpet. The twins fetched their violins and the elderly couple clapped in time.

Her yard filled with singing, humming, tootling people. It was growing dark, but still it was warm for February. Terry flipped on the porch light, creating a cozy glow in the deepening dusk.

Karen joined in on the tambourine as they blared and banged their way through "Camptown Races," "The Ants Go Marching One by One," "Seventy-six Trombones" and "Whistle a Happy Tune," which was accompanied by the most cacophonous assortment of whistling ever heard outside a teapot factory.

The sky had turned blue-black by the time people scattered to their homes. "Can't say when I've had so much fun," commented Mr. Rivers as he blew spittle out of his trumpet.

"Ought to do more of this," agreed the elderly gentleman. "Good old-fashioned fun."

Terry helped Lou resettle his one-man band in his pickup truck while Karen got the children ready for bed. They slipped into slumber without protest, Bopper humming tunelessly under his breath.

Karen and Terry adjourned to the den. "Things just seem to happen around you," she said. "I feel as if leprechauns might pop out of the woodwork."

"I'd like that," he said.

"You told me I knew how to make a home." She rested her head against the arm of the couch. "Well, you seem to know how to make a neighborhood."

"Circuses run in the family." His thumb traced the line of her jaw. "Care to try for a high-wire act?"

"Without a net?" she murmured, drawing closer.

"Flying trapeze and all." His mouth came down on hers. Karen had barely begun exploring his lips when he caught her shoulders and lowered her on the cushions, his hard body poised above her.

"What—?"

"I need you." Terry's voice rasped with a mixture of surprise and passion. "It just hit me."

"Like a ton of bricks." That was the last observation Karen had time to make.

This was a new Terry, ringmaster and acrobat rolled into one. Arching above her, he claimed her mouth and throat as his hands deftly parted her blouse. Karen could barely assimilate the sensations all at once: the firm insistence of his thigh as he parted her legs, the pressure of his thumbs hardening her nipples, the wet teasing of his tongue on the inner coil of her ear.

She swung high above the world, aware only of Terry, responding to his signals. They flew together, tossed each other, defied gravity. They met on the highest arc of the trapeze. He united them with the gentle power of an athlete, intensifying his rhythms as they rocketed through the air.

Karen heard herself calling his name. Asking for more. Letting go, soaring without a net, clinging to Terry as he thrust her all the way to the top.

Passion rioted through her, so intense it wiped away time and space. She met his wild demands with her own until they let go of the trapeze and flew, wild and free, to the utmost peak of the big top, and then drifted down again.

By SIX-THIRTY on Thursday night, Terry had cleaned up the supper dishes and the children were playing Hungry Hungry Hippos in the den. He sat down with them. The game was childishly simple: there were four hippo heads around the edges of a game board, and you snapped their mouths to capture little white marbles.

Bopper kept winning, to Rose's frustration and Terry's amazement. He couldn't seem to get the hang of the thing. Humiliated by a five year old.

The problem was, he couldn't stop checking his watch. The hands were edging toward seven. Soon it would be time to leave for his critique group. If, of course, he had been planning to go.

"Terry," Rose said. "You're kicking the couch."

"Nervous energy." He stopped poking the sofa.

"Let's watch a video." He made popcorn and they settled down, as if attending a real movie.

An hour later, Terry noticed the children nodding off, so he took them upstairs.

As he read their story, he wondered if Joni and Mitch were at the critique group tonight. He could picture his friends sitting down together and exchanging insights.

He needed their feedback to jump start his book. He knew he was losing enthusiasm and it worried him.

When Bopper had been tucked in, Rose sat up in bed. "You're the best baby-sitter we ever had."

Terry squeezed her.

"Your popcorn is terrific," she murmured against his shoulder.

"I consider that high praise indeed." He could hear her contented sigh as he strolled out of the room.

Chapter Twelve

Helene stood on the clubhouse terrace overlooking the condo swimming pool. A March breeze ruffled her hair and fluttered the white wedding ribbons woven through the railing.

Below, Rose and Bopper cavorted in the water as Karen watched from the sidelines. The children had shed their good clothes, but Karen still wore her lavender matron-of-honor dress. She looked young for thirty—it was hard to believe she'd juggled heavy responsibilities for so many years.

As Helene watched, that nice man, Terry, walked up with four glasses of punch and stole a quick kiss.

He and her daughter had clearly become more than roommates. Helene hadn't lived for more than half a century with her head in a barrel.

Once upon a time, she might have tried to engineer a marriage. It was surprising how easily one could manipulate people—asking for favors that would throw them together; arranging for Terry to drive her somewhere, perhaps, and using the occasion to drop hints.

Karen deserved a good marriage, and Helene hoped to see it happen. But this past year or so, she'd decided to stop living her life through others. To stop depending on them and trying to make them responsible for her happiness.

Goodness! What an awkward time for self-examination, at her own wedding.

Helene turned toward the clubhouse. Two huge sprays of flowers bordered the doorway. Indoors, a floral centerpiece dominated the buffet table, corsages bloomed on some of her friends' blouses and even Frederick wore a carnation in his buttonhole. Helene felt as if she'd been married in a garden.

"The ceremony was lovely!" Emma, a friend from Helene's gardening club, stopped by with a plateful of wedding cake. "What a perfect setting! And the minister—he said such sweet things."

"I don't know about the golden-years part." Helene smiled. "I'm only fifty-four."

"Really? We always think of you as...I mean you..." Emma's words trailed off in confusion.

"My first husband was fifteen years older than me," Helene said. "I suppose I identified with his age group more than my own."

"Well, you don't look it!" Emma recovered her composure. "You make a stunning bride. What a perfect shade of pink!"

"Thank you." Helene brushed a leaf off her skirt. She'd searched for days to find this dress, an understated creation of silk with a flattering high neck and a scarf hemline.

"Mind if I join you?" Frederick slipped an arm around his wife's waist.

Helene rested her head against his shoulder. He was such a strong man. Yet not overwhelming, as Boyce, her first husband, had been.

Boyce had insisted on taking charge of everything, and as a young woman Helene had liked that fine. Raised with an overbearing mother and timid father, she'd cringed from life's demands. Cranky clerks scared her, bank statements stirred waves of anxiety, every time she tried to learn to drive, she'd become so fearful she could hardly breathe.

In her late forties Helene had gone through what people called the change of life, but the real change had occurred about a year ago.

Karen's divorce had shaken up Helene's cozy world. Soon afterward she'd run into Frederick and realized that if she tried to cling she would lose him.

Funny how she could trace the change to one particular incident on one particular day thirteen months ago. It had seemed so minor at the time.

The battery in her watch needed replacing. Helene took it to a discount store. A friendly clerk told her the batteries were out of stock and named other stores that carried them.

"Don't pay more than five dollars," the woman had advised. "We charge about three-fifty."

Helene took the bus to another store, where a stern-faced jeweler picked up the watch without comment, pried it open and stuck in a battery.

"That will be eight dollars," he said.

"Eight dollars?" Helene wondered what she should do. The difference wasn't really that much, but she lived on a tight budget. Her husband's insurance had been augmented ten years ago by a small inheritance from her mother, but it still didn't amount to a lot.

The main thing was, she didn't like getting ripped off.

The jeweler tapped his fingers on the counter and stared toward an approaching customer. The message was clear—Come On, Lady, I Haven't Got All Day.

"Take it out," she said.

"Excuse me?" His eyes focused on her at last.

"Eight dollars is excessive." Helene gripped her purse tightly for moral support.

"I've already opened the package." He indicated the cardboard-and-plastic packet.

"I don't care," Helene heard herself say. "Take it out."

He gave her a dirty look, but he obeyed. Helene marched away, only discovering as she reached the bus stop that she was shaking.

She'd gone to another store, where she had a battery installed for four dollars. She used her savings to purchase some juicy pork chops for Frederick.

She never told him why she was in a mood for celebrating that night. It seemed so trivial. But that day marked the beginning of the change.

In the past year, Helene had lost her fear of traveling. She'd learned to drive, and found that she enjoyed it. She'd changed doctors because the old one kept her waiting. She'd organized this wedding all by herself, with only a little help from Frederick.

Now Helene stood tall in the sunlight, side by side with her husband. Ready for a new life and whatever it might bring.

She decided the minister's reference to golden years hadn't been so inappropriate, after all.

DESPITE HELENE'S protests, Sid, Marian, Karen and Terry insisted on cleaning up the clubhouse after the guests left. Frederick escorted the children to the playground, from which Helene could hear them shouting happily.

She sat on the terrace drinking a glass of champagne and allowing herself to relax. The recent weeks had been a whirlwind, lining up the photographer and the caterer, choosing a dress and decorations and flowers. It felt good to sit here and do nothing.

"Done with that?" Terry quirked an eyebrow as he reached for her empty glass. He towed a plastic bag full of plates and cups.

"Sit down," Helene said. "Keep me company."

He edged onto a seat opposite her. Despite his friendliness, she always sensed a reserve in Terry. Something held him back from Karen, and while Helene knew it was none of her business, she wished she could help.

"Karen tells me you've been baby-sitting on Thursday nights these past three weeks," she said. "I think that's wonderful. Men didn't used to do these things when my children were small."

"I like the kids." He jiggled the trash bag, settling the contents.

"She's concerned about your missing your writers' group. I hope it hasn't been too much of a problem." Helene knew she shouldn't probe like this. Hadn't she sworn not to manipulate people any more?

"I've missed it," Terry admitted. "I'm kind of stuck on this book I'm writing. I guess I need inspiration. Being around other writers might help."

Helene forced herself to keep silent. Terry could talk if he wanted, but she wouldn't pry further.

"I can't let her give up her class." He let out a long breath. "The assignments have been a real challenge and she's putting so much effort into it."

The conflict in his eyes touched her. This man must really care for Karen.

"I get restless when I have to live up to other people's expectations." Terry tossed a crumb to a foraging pigeon. "It's a failing of mine."

"You seem to be overcoming it." Helene refused to let herself say more.

"I used to be this obnoxiously perfect little kid." Terry's eyes took on a faraway look. "Mr. Prim and Proper. The other kids made fun of me. It hurt, but I didn't know what to do. My grandmother was very strict."

He had undergone a transition, he told Helene, which he called The Day I Stopped Being Perfect. His father's circus had been in town, and ten-year-old Terry had stayed up late, reveling in the smell of elephants and greasepaint, playing with the clowns and flirting with the lady who performed tricks on horseback.

The next morning he'd returned to his hard wooden desk and the snide remarks. One boy in particular tormented him, throwing paper wads when the teacher's back was turned and making rude noises as Terry passed his table at lunch.

Without planning it, Terry swung around and spilled his milk over the boy's head. In the shocked silence that followed, he issued a stream of apologies while dumping a plateful of chicken cacciatore and a slice of apple pie into the tormentor's lap.

The laughter of classmates buoyed him along to the principal's office. This time, the laughter was on Terry's side. From that day forward, he kept it that way.

A lump formed in Helene's throat. She understood Terry better now, and she admired him for trying to be the kind of man Karen needed. The class clown, un-learning a lesson he'd absorbed so many years ago.

He was far more mature than Bobby. Still, it was too soon to tell whether he'd eventually explode from the constraints, a jack-in-the-box to the end.

Was Karen making the same mistake twice?

"I guess it sounds silly, making a big deal out of dumping milk over some dweeb's head," Terry said. "It's not as if I endured a terrible trauma."

"Loneliness can be traumatic," Helene said.

Their gazes met in an instant of shared understanding. Then she heard the voices of her grown children floating toward them.

"Time to go," Terry said. "You're a good listener. And in case I forgot to say it earlier, best wishes. I wish you every happiness."

"Thanks." Helene stood up when he did. "Go make my daughter laugh. But if you get mad at her, don't you dare spill anything on that dress."

"Haven't done it in years." Terry held his hand up as if taking an oath, then went to join Karen.

A tall figure slipped into place behind Helene. "Let's go somewhere alone," Frederick's voice murmured close to her ear. "I'll put on some soft music, we'll turn down the lights..."

"Goodbye, everybody!" Helene called and dashed away, her arm through her husband's.

"I'VE ALWAYS WANTED to explore this place." Terry led Karen down a walkway from the street. It ran between two houses, separated from the lawns by a high hedge.

"Are you sure we're not intruding?" She glanced at the large modern houses tucked neatly along the street. "This has to be private property."

"Belongs to the community association," he said. "Lou gave us permission, remember?"

Going for a walk in what Terry referred to as "the ditch" wasn't exactly what Karen had had in mind for a rare child-free day.

Helene and Frederick had taken the children to Disneyland. Although the wedding was only a week behind them, the couple had scheduled their honeymoon for April and were roving around Southern California during March. Exploring their own backyard, as they'd put it.

Well, this might be somebody's backyard, but it wasn't hers, Karen reflected as the sidewalk ended and she found herself scooting down a steep slope behind Terry. The dirt path cut between tall, slim trees amid a blanket of leaves. Turning around, she could look into several yards—one equipped with a spa and another with a playhouse. Otherwise, the trees blocked off all sign of civilization.

Lou Loomis was out of town and had asked them to feed his dog. While they were visiting his house here in Brea, half an hour's drive from Karen's home, Terry had insisted they take this hike. He'd made it sound like a fantasy adventure.

Thank goodness she'd worn jogging shoes, Karen told herself as she half slid down behind Terry. The slope bottomed out in what was unmistakably a drainage channel, the banks formed of rock clumps and dirt. On the far side a steep grade led up to the budding trees of what had once, predevelopment, been a commercial avocado grove.

"I'm surprised you don't live in a community like this," she told Terry. "Oldtown Whittier is so—funky."

"That's why I like it." He took her hand to help her over a log as they set out along the narrow gully. The contact reminded Karen of the things she'd rather be doing today.

"This is beautiful." She had to admit the interplay of light and shadow and the flash of a squirrel through the bushes were worth watching. On the other hand, enough was enough. "I especially like the beer bottle over there."

"Endangered species." Terry peered to their left. "I understand there's a lost bridge somewhere. Haven't you always wanted to find a lost bridge?"

He continued picking his way along the drainage ditch. Karen hurried to keep up.

"How lost could it be?" she asked. "These houses can't be more than a dozen years old."

"Karen." Terry turned to face her, blocking the path. "Ground rules. When we're having an adventure, we search out possibilities. We push the envelope of our imagination. We ignore minor inconveniences."

"And boldly go where no one has been so stupid as to go before," she said.

He laughed, bent down, caught her chin in his hand and kissed her.

On the unseen street above, a trash truck churned by. Karen and Terry jumped apart.

"Ignore that." He drew close again. "It must have been one of the evil sorcerer's destructo beasts."

"The evil sorcerer's destructo beasts?" Karen muttered. "Look, Terry..."

He didn't try to kiss her again. "I'm not turning back until we find the lost bridge."

Part of her wanted to let go of her adult inhibitions and play games with Terry. Another part stood aside muttering about mud on her shoes and broken glass in the channel.

"Okay," she said. "Let's go for it."

They picked their way between sheer banks ten feet high. Water trickled down the ditch, but it had been a dry month and this looked like nothing more than lawn-watering runoff.

Karen balanced and leaped from rock to rock, letting Terry hand her over a few difficult gaps. It wasn't really rough going, but a challenge to keep her shoes from turning into globs of mud.

They came to a tunnel that ran beneath a cross street. Karen recognized it as the road that connected the housing development to the outside world. Even here, though, she couldn't see the main streets on either side of them, although she heard the faint whir of a car going by.

"The lost bridge?" she said hopefully.

Terry shook his head. "The troll's tunnel. Look sharp now."

They were halfway through the tunnel when he flattened her against one side.

"Uh-oh," Karen said. "Is this where I pay the troll?"

"The very same." His hands gripped her waist. "Fair maiden, I claim thee."

"Will you take a rain check?" She felt his breath tickle her neck. "I mean, a drain check?"

He threw his head back and laughed. "Since you put it that way, yes."

They proceeded between more high banks. The sense of isolation deepened. Karen marveled to find that the

high embankments and the trees could so effectively
screen out the world.

She was enjoying the hike so much that when at last
they passed beneath a wooden footbridge, she was relieved to hear Terry declare that it was the wrong one.
Not lost at all, but a much used connection between the
houses and the tennis courts, which lay off to their
right.

As if to verify his claim, she spotted a faded yellow
tennis ball lying ahead in the ditch. "Somebody's aim
must be off."

Terry put out an arm to stop her. "Wait. It looks
like—yes—a dropping from the sorcerer's monstrous
Roc."

"That's not a rock," she said.

"Roc. A fabulous bird." He frowned. "It can penetrate even this hidden passage."

Something else had penetrated, too, judging by the
shards of brown glass. A beer-guzzling gargoyle, no
doubt.

"We must traverse onward," Terry said.

"I don't know." Now that she'd seen the glass,
Karen felt less eager to explore the winding channel
ahead. "I don't think there is any lost bridge."

He quirked an eyebrow, reminding her that their
"prime directive" required making the best of things,
and led the way. Farther along, the channel deepened.
Karen overcame a momentary twinge of claustropho-
bia, seeing the banks loom dozens of feet high on either side.

They turned a corner and she saw it, a rickety structure spanning the ditch ahead. Part of its support had
broken off, and no path led to or away from it.

"That's it!" Terry caught her hand in excitement and half pulled, half guided her up a series of footholds until they'd reached the base of the bridge.

"Do you think it's safe?" She scraped mud off her shoes and regarded the structure dubiously.

"I'll check it." He bounded onto the span and jumped up and down. Karen's heart bounded into her throat. The wood groaned but held.

"You're certifiable." She followed him onto the bridge. "What if you'd fallen?"

Instead of answering, he pointed straight ahead. "Look! There!"

From this height, she could see that the ditch widened and embraced a pool. A raccoon was drinking, its ringed tail fluffed out behind. It peered around and then dipped a shiny object into the water.

"The magic ring!" Terry whispered. "That must be one of the good witch's familiars!"

The raccoon caught sight of them. It rose on its hind legs, sharp snout testing the air. As if by design, it set the shiny object in the mud and whisked away through the bushes.

"Let's go!" Terry raced down from the bridge, slipping and sliding into the channel. Karen followed more cautiously, to find him inspecting the raccoon's treasure, a scratched shooting marble.

Inside the clear glass glinted a blue cat's-eye.

"The good witch can see us," Terry breathed. "She knows we've come."

"What happens now?" Karen had forgotten about muddy jogging shoes and sore muscles.

"We take this home and keep it safe," he said. "Where the sorcerer will never find it."

"Bopper's sock drawer," she suggested.

"The tower. Perfect." Terry studied the pond. "Too bad we must have scared off the mermaids."

Karen reached for the marble. "It really is pretty. I haven't had one of these since I was a child."

She found herself cradled against him. "You're a good sport, Karen."

"So are you." In the dappled sunlight, she gazed up at Terry. He had a smudge of dirt on his cheek like an overgrown kid. She loved this free-spirited side of him. She would never want to turn him into a button-down executive type, the kind most people thought of as husband material.

Stay free, she thought. *But stay with me.*

Their kiss was long and tender. A bird sang somewhere in the trees. A squirrel came down to drink at the pool, and meandered on its way.

"Let's go home." Terry took Karen's hand to help her back to the bridge. "We can walk along the street up there."

"Terry." She could see now that she'd been testing him this past month. Maybe he'd been testing her just a little bit today. They'd both passed. "You've missed enough writers' meetings. I'll hire a baby-sitter."

"No." He shook his head. "*I'll* hire a baby-sitter."

It seemed like the perfect compromise.

MITCH MARAKIAN read from his latest mystery, holding the critique group rapt. He had a keen grasp of characterization, and Terry found himself intrigued as always by Mitch's series detective, a trash collector who followed clues found in garbage cans.

It was an unlikely premise, but the public loved it. Terry could see why. Tonight's chapter dealt with a body found stuffed into a Dumpster. The victim was a drug dealer—or had he been framed to look like one?

Yet all the while Terry was listening, something nagged at the back of his mind. His thoughts kept straying. He couldn't help wondering...

Was the baby-sitter letting Bopper drink too much apple juice? He'd wet his bed for sure.

Was she paying enough attention to Rose? Bopper tended to monopolize people's attention, but his sister had needs, too.

Had Terry remembered to lock the back door? He'd cleaned the chinchilla cage earlier and taken out the shavings. Surely he'd secured everything, but he couldn't clearly remember turning the key in the lock.

What if it was open? What if...?

He managed to endure his doubts through the first two readers and excused himself at the break. He told his fellow writers that the sitter was new and shouldn't be left with the kids too long.

The truth was, Karen had used the same girl before on numerous occasions and trusted her completely.

What was happening to him? Terry wondered. He'd never felt torn in half like this, worrying without cause about what might be happening somewhere else. This was exactly the kind of stress he'd tried to avoid.

That was the sneaky thing about commitment, Terry reflected as he chafed at a red light and wondered if the baby-sitter had thought to brush Bopper's teeth.

Commitment wasn't something other people imposed on you from outside. It grew from within. The way it had grown inside him, without his realizing it.

He parked in front of the house and raced inside. The baby-sitter was coming down the stairs.

"I just checked," she said. "They're both asleep."

Terry paid her and watched out the front door as the teenager walked to her home down the block. Back inside, he double-checked on the children and then settled down with the newspaper.

The children might be fine, but his little world wasn't safe yet. Not until Karen got home. As he'd done since she began her class, he would wait up for her.

Terry leaned back, thinking about the fun they'd had on their adventure walk. Thinking about how well they meshed, how much they'd become attuned to each other.

Karen would be too tired for a serious discussion tonight. But the first chance he got, Terry had something important to ask her.

Chapter Thirteen

Karen sat in the den, visualizing her office-management class. She didn't know why she felt so nervous.

A presentation. Big deal. It wasn't as if Karen suffered from more than a normal amount of stage fright. After shepherding two children around all these years, she knew how to plant herself center stage and make herself heard.

For some reason, that thought didn't make her feel any better.

Her task was to interview and assess a job candidate, who would be portrayed by the teacher, Mrs. Sayles. Karen knew that the applicant's answers would be full of booby traps for her and she must prepare well.

She stretched, feeling the strain of a long Wednesday at work, followed by a rush to deliver the kids to a birthday party, and then by two hours of concentrated study.

From upstairs came the steady thump-thump of the rowing machine. Terry had been at it for an hour. She suspected he was fighting off a tendency to pop in on her every five minutes, and she appreciated it.

Karen checked her notes. She'd written out her questions, and how she would handle some curveballs the teacher might throw. She planned to test the "candidate" on some of the office machines and to verify credentials. Plus she'd need to provide the right amount of encouragement if the applicant seemed promising.

Their grade in the course was based on their work in these presentations—Mrs. Sayles had told them from the beginning that she considered exams worthless in a class such as this. Karen agreed.

Maybe that was why she felt so nervous. Grades. She hadn't had to face that kind of evaluation in more than ten years.

It didn't help to recall the previous week, when another student had been assigned to explain his office procedures to his boss. Mrs. Sayles had shredded his presentation, even though it had initially struck Karen as well done.

She stretched, feeling little knots uncramp in her neck and shoulders, and turned back to her notes. The handwriting blurred. No way to concentrate any more tonight.

She'd arranged to leave work a couple of hours early tomorrow, before class. Since her tirade about working unpaid overtime, George had been more careful about his demands and had agreed to some compensatory time off.

The rowing machine went right on thumping. Karen felt a twinge of guilt, but she wasn't in the mood for conversation.

She closed her notebook and tiptoed upstairs. A neighbor had offered to drop the kids off about nine when she fetched her own children. That left time for a long, lovely shower.

The hot water pelted Karen's neck and shoulders like tiny fingers. She closed her eyes and concentrated on the marvelous warmth.

Rivulets traced her throat and breasts, dropping to her thighs. She remembered the pool she and Terry had found in the drainage channel and imagined it transformed into an enchanted pond. A mermaid's pond. Karen stretched. A mermaid, bathing in a waterfall...

The glass door creaked open. She looked up to see Terry drop the towel from around his waist and step in beside her.

"Terrific idea," he said.

"Hey!" Karen couldn't help laughing. "Who invited you?"

"Save water, shower with a friend," he reminded her.

"All in the name of water conservation," she murmured as her arms encircled him. She could feel the strength in his back as she rubbed it. "That rowing machine does wonders."

"This shower does wonders." Terry caught her hips against his. Karen felt the naked length of him as the pulsing water pressed her closer, enclosing them in a steamy cocoon.

Did a mermaid revealing herself to a handsome sailor feel this same aching need? Would she tease him this way with her lips and breasts, stroking him and then retreating? Would he chase her inch by inch through her slippery world, chuckling and moaning and cornering her at last?

She wondered if a mermaid felt the same delicious satisfaction when she opened herself to her sailor, when he filled her at last. The world was transformed into steam and hunger, two bodies drenched in desire, and an eager thrusting that aroused rivers of pleasure.

Warm water dripped around Terry and sluiced onto Karen's face as he leaned above her.

She surged over the waterfall, carrying him with her. A wild ride, a fantastic ride through a landscape of silver and scarlet. When at last they floated in the lazy pool, Karen let contentment seep through her.

It must be nearly time for the children to come home. She sighed and wriggled free.

Dried and robed, she was brushing her hair in the bedroom when Terry appeared over her shoulder. He looked rakishly handsome in striped pajamas.

"I've been thinking." He sat on the edge of the bed. "Well, more than thinking. Pondering."

In the pause that followed, Karen wondered what he had in mind. Another expedition into the ditch? A band performance with Lou Loomis at a public park? With Terry, you could never tell.

"Will you marry me?" he said.

Karen paused with her brush in midair. Seconds ticked by. She had to remind herself to breathe.

Yes, Terry! You make me laugh, you make me feel things I didn't know I was capable of. You've given the children such happiness.

Why couldn't she say it?

"Have you thought about..." She paused. "I mean..."

"Am I ready to handle this?" he finished for her. "I think so, Karen. It's not a step either of us takes lightly."

"I love you." She whispered the words. It had been so long since she'd said them to a man. So long since she'd wanted to say them.

She still couldn't give him an answer.

What was she waiting for? Did she expect Terry to be transformed into Father Knows Best? He'd asked her to marry him. He wanted to share his life with her. And she could admit to herself at last that she felt the same way.

There was, however, one lesson the years had taught Karen. *Sleep on it.*

"I think the answer will be yes, but I need a little time. Can I tell you tomorrow?"

"I guess I took you by surprise," Terry said.

"That's putting it mildly." Karen turned to face him. "I have to be sure this is the right time for me."

"And for the children," he said.

"Are you including yourself?"

His grin broke the tension. "I guess playing the romantic hero still doesn't come naturally. I'm trying to picture myself as a groom. A real, verifiable grown-up."

"You do own a tuxedo," Karen pointed out.

"And I do love the bride." He caught himself. "The maybe bride."

She was considering saying yes right now, and to hell with common sense, when the doorbell rang.

"Back to reality," he said.

They walked downstairs together, separating just before they reached the front door.

TERRY REALIZED ON Thursday morning that it was going to be a long day.

Not a painfully long day, unless you counted the overworked muscles in his chest, which he chose to ignore. He actually caught himself whistling once or twice.

He sat at his computer keyboard thinking about Karen. Trying out the words "wife," "husband" and "Mrs. Vogel." He wondered if Karen would want to change her name and decided it didn't matter.

They could get married at her church. Maybe she would prefer her mother's clubhouse or their own backyard.

He didn't care if they eloped to Las Vegas, as long as it was legal.

When the phone rang midmorning, his heart whammed into a fast tango. Karen couldn't wait. She'd called to tell him yes, yes, yes, yes, yes....

"Hello?" He tried to play it cool.

It was his editor. She never said her name, but she had a distinctive New York accent and a cheerful lilt to her voice. "Terry! I have some wonderful news!"

"Perfect timing," he said. "I'm getting married, myself." He wondered if he was taking too much for granted and decided he didn't care.

"Then you'll understand!"

"Understand what?"

"I'm pregnant!" she said. "I'm going on leave next month."

"Great." But it wasn't great. The loony bins were full of writers whose books had been orphaned when an editor moved on, leaving them in the hands of newcomers who didn't care whether those books lived or died. "What about my book?"

"It might have to be postponed a while longer," she said. "Things will be a little hectic around here. One of the other editors will be covering for me until they find a temporary replacement. But don't worry. *Ghoul of the Golden West* is so fantastic, it will sell itself."

That was an expression Terry appreciated about as much as "We're going to have to audit your last five tax returns." No book sold itself. If it wasn't in the bookstores and nobody had ever heard of it, how could they buy it?

"I gotta go now," his editor said. "Congratulations to you, too!" Click.

Terry flipped a switch. The bright green type on his computer narrowed to a thin line and vanished. He realized then that he hadn't saved his file and he'd just lost a page and a half of manuscript.

It hardly mattered. He'd been writing himself in circles with *Dream a Little Scream*, anyway.

He wished there really were monsters. He wished slimy things with fangs and warts lived in the closets of New York publishers and jumped on editors who pushed back your publication date, then got pregnant and orphaned you to the whims of fate.

She probably wouldn't even invite him to the baby shower.

Terry went out for a walk. When he came back, the light was blinking on his answering machine.

With a sense of dread, he played back the message.

It was his agent. "Terry, hello? Just got a call from Joe Lancer. He's anxious to see a copy of *Golden West* so I'm sending it out today. Bad news on the option. He's shopped *Major League* all over town and no takers. Don't worry. Another year or two and horror will make a comeback. Gotta go."

Terry rewound the tape and set the machine to reprogram his announcement. "This is Terry," he said.

"If you're an editor calling with good news, dial one. If you're my agent, dial two. If this is bad news, this message will self-destruct."

He switched off the announcement tape and didn't even bother to listen to it.

Terry wandered down to the laundry room and fed the chinchillas. The babies were growing rapidly. He wondered if there really was money in chinchilla ranching and decided he wouldn't have the heart. He couldn't save the house with blood money.

He knew how this was going to look to Karen and he couldn't think of a damn thing to do about it.

"Everything set for the realtors' preview?" George asked when he got back from lunch.

"Coffee maker's ready to go, and I'll pick up doughnuts on the way," Karen assured him. "I'll get it all set out for you before I leave."

"Leave?" he said.

George had listed a sharp house in La Habra Heights, priced at $535,000. With a commission like that in the balance, he was bending over backward to find a buyer.

This afternoon, he'd scheduled an open house for other real-estate agents to "preview" the property. That way they'd have it in mind if they came upon a likely buyer.

"Remember? I arranged two weeks ago to take this afternoon off," Karen said. "I put a reminder note on your desk. I have to make a presentation in class tonight."

Irritation wrinkled his forehead. "Yes, yes. But it's my wife's birthday. I promised to take her shopping."

"The stores will be open tonight," Karen said.

"We're having a party. I promised her some new earrings, and if I don't go along she'll buy the Hope Diamond." George strode toward the exit. "It's over at five. You'll have plenty of time to get to your class."

"But I'm not prepared!" Karen said. "I was counting on this afternoon."

"Then uncount on it." He was halfway out the door already.

Karen picked up her purse. "You'd better be heading to the property, George. Because I'm not going to be there."

"Now, look." He swung around. "If you want to take a class, I don't care. What you do in your spare time is none of my business. When you're at work, however..."

"I cleared it with you in advance." Karen fought to keep calm. "I could understand the problem if you had some big client dangling. But you just went ahead and scheduled something that could have been done yesterday or the day before."

"It wouldn't have been Irene's birthday," he said. "Karen, you'll handle that realtor's preview—or don't bother coming back."

Deep inside her, something snapped. "Goodbye, George." She stood in front of the door until he stepped aside, disbelief written across his face.

"I mean it," he said.

"So do I." Karen felt his glare boring into her back as she stalked to her car. She couldn't give in. She couldn't bear to work for George any longer under these circumstances.

Halfway home, she still fought to catch her breath. What had she done?

Thank goodness she had Terry to lean on.

HE WASN'T HOME when she arrived. Karen had trouble concentrating on her studies, but she focused on the satisfaction of finally standing up to George and managed to put together a presentation.

Terry arrived with the kids as she was leaving for class. Karen explained about the dinner she'd left in the refrigerator and raced out the door.

Terry hadn't seemed as bouncy as usual, she thought as she clicked down the walkway. Had he sensed her own mood?

On the long drive to class, she debated what to do next. She wasn't even sure if she qualified for unemployment insurance. Had she quit or been fired?

In class, the presentation was scheduled first thing. Mrs. Sayles strode in with a portfolio, assuming the role of a know-it-all interviewee.

After the disruptions of the day, Karen found that a crisp take-charge attitude came easily. She brushed aside the applicant's swaggering. Mrs. Sayles, playing a semiobnoxious character, tried to seize control of the interview several times, but Karen calmly and firmly prevented it.

"Very good," the teacher said when they were finished.

Karen took a deep breath. She wasn't sure she'd explained the office hierarchy clearly, but it didn't seem to matter.

"I'm very pleased with the change in your approach," the teacher said. "You've always been rather tentative, Karen. This was an improvement."

"Good," Karen said. "Because I need to find a new job in a hurry."

"I'll write you a recommendation." Mrs. Sayles steered the class into a discussion of how to handle a difficult interviewee, pointing out several times how well Karen had stayed on top.

She felt good about her success. She felt even better about getting a recommendation.

She was going to need it.

THE HANDS OF HER watch had crept past eleven when Karen reached home. Terry was sitting up in the living room.

She realized with a start that she hadn't given his proposal any thought today. The most important step in her life, and it had flown right out of her mind.

"Oh, Terry," she said. "I know I promised you an answer..."

"That's okay." His voice sagged with weariness. "You see, Karen—"

"I lost my—"

"They're not renewing the option on my book."

"What option?" She tried to break through the buzz in her brain. "I thought the rights were sold."

"I... sort of gave the wrong impression," he said.

Karen sat on a chair. Terry watched her from the edge of the couch.

"I don't understand."

Terry told her about his editor and the producer. "Of course, I've still got royalties and subsidiary rights. Enough to get by."

Karen tried to add things up and couldn't. "The house," she said. "How did you pay for the house?"

"I borrowed the money from Mitch." Terry let out a deep breath. "I promised to pay it back. In a year."

"All of it?"

"Most of it. I'd saved up a big down payment, but even so..." Terry shook his head. "A bank would never give me a loan, the way my income seesaws from year to year."

Losing the house didn't bother Karen nearly as much as the fact that Terry had lied. She realized he hadn't meant any harm. He'd just gotten caught up in his fantasies.

But like so many times with Bobby, it was she and the kids who would have to suffer the results.

"I've been thinking about this all day," he said. "There is one possibility."

She leaned forward.

"You could loan me the money. You did make some profit from the sale, didn't you? And you've mentioned a fund for the children." Terry hurried on before she could respond. "I'm not asking you to spend your nest egg. It would be a formal loan, and I'd make payments. Consider it an investment."

Maybe it was exhaustion or the events of the day, but tears sprang to Karen's eyes. "Terry, I—I lost my job today."

"Oh." His blue eyes got cloudy, as if a veil had fallen. "I'm sorry."

Karen retreated toward the staircase. If she stayed here any longer she might break down. "Good night, Terry."

"Look, Karen, we'll figure this out. Something always turns up." He sounded more downhearted than she'd ever heard him.

Karen checked on the children and got ready for bed. She could hear Terry moving about in his room, and had to check the impulse to go to him.

The trust between them had been shaken tonight. Only time would tell if they could put things straight again. She hoped he was right, that something really would turn up.

Chapter Fourteen

The Whittier Boomers.

It sounded like a basketball team or a club for yuppies, Karen mused as she emerged from her car and smoothed her skirt.

But she'd heard of them. Who in the real-estate business hadn't?

She tugged on twisted panty hose and tried to absorb the events of the past twenty-four hours. Things had moved so fast, she felt as if she'd switched time zones and forgotten to reset her watch.

After spending the weekend putting together a resumé, she'd gone to an employment agency yesterday. A counselor had interviewed her with cool efficiency and Karen walked out wondering if she'd ever hear from the woman again.

An hour later, the counselor called with this appointment.

Karen stared up at the corner building with its fresh coat of sky blue paint. The sign read, "The Whittier Boomers, Real-estate Experts."

This was no one-man operation in a storefront office. The Whittier Boomers employed forty-three agents and a clerical staff of five. Actually, at the moment, there were four. And one vacancy.

Karen swallowed an attack of the jitters. She knew she'd fit right in if there were an opening for receptionist or clerk-typist. But office manager? What did she think she was doing?

Best not to dwell on it, or she might chicken out.

She marched up to the French double doors and pushed them open.

A girl of about nineteen sat polishing her nails behind a built-in counter with a nameplate that said Tiffany. "Yes?"

"I'm here for my interview with Mrs. Blankenship. I'm Karen Loesser."

"Uh, yeah." Tiffany blew on her nails. "About the job, huh?" The phone rang. The girl picked it up between her thumb and forefinger. "Yeah. Hi. Whittier Boomers."

It took ten minutes to pry Tiffany loose and send her in search of the broker. No one covered the phones while she was gone—one line rang ten times before it stopped. If there were three other clerical employees, where were they?

When at last she was ushered into Mrs. Blankenship's office, Karen found it to be as big as her own living room, tastefully decorated in pinks and beiges with Danish modern furniture. Karen liked it, or as much as she could make out beneath the piles of documents, files, memos and newspaper ads.

Mrs. Blankenship herself was a tall, almost gaunt woman with imposing hair. She seemed distracted as she introduced herself, and explained, "I've got an escrow blowing up, I'm afraid."

"You're involved in sales yourself?" Karen asked in surprise.

"My old clients keep popping up and I can't resist a commission. By the way, everybody calls me Beverly." Mrs. Blankenship tapped her fingers on the desk. "I'm expecting a call from a loan officer. I can't understand..." She took out her beeper and pressed the Test button. It shrilled with ear-splitting volume. "Oh, good. I was afraid the batteries had gone dead."

"Could you tell me about the job?" Karen prodded.

"Oh. Oh, yes." Beverly forced her attention back to the interview.

The office manager was, of course, supposed to supervise the staff, Mrs. Blankenship told her. Also to make sure the realtors didn't monopolize the secretaries with their private needs—they were expected to hire their own assistants, if necessary—and generally run interference.

"We've had terrible turnover," Mrs. Blankenship said. "Both in the manager's job and on the clerical staff. Hardly anyone sticks around longer than six months, except for Nina. She's been here for ages, but she can't seem to get the hang of the fax and the computers. I can't fire her. She's the only one who knows how to keep the books."

This didn't sound promising.

However, when she asked about the salary, she was pleasantly surprised to find it half again as much as George paid.

"How soon can you start?" Beverly spared an anxious glance at her silent beeper. "Darn this lender. He's the one who screwed up the deal. He'd better call me, or I'll never bring him any business again. Would tomorrow be all right?''

Karen decided it was best not to sound too eager. "How about next Monday?"

"Fine. I'll have Nina put you on the payroll," Beverly said just as a beep-beep-beep filled the room. "Thank goodness." Karen wasn't sure whether the broker was thanking goodness for being paged or for hiring a new office manager, and she didn't much care.

She had a job!

TERRY MET JONI RODD for lunch at McDonald's. Today was something known as child-free day at the school, and she was able to get away for an hour.

She ordered a salad and a diet drink. He ordered a Happy Meal and made sure they didn't forget the toy.

"It's for the kids," he said as they sat down, but he couldn't resist opening the cellophane packet and working the tiny robot's arms and legs.

"What's the emergency?" Joni asked.

He filled Joni in on the situation. "What a mess," he concluded as he downed a McNugget. "I never figured my publisher *and* my producer would let me down. The worst part is, they've let Karen down, too."

He waited, with a sense of raw injustice, for Joni's healing sympathy.

"They haven't let Karen down," she said. "You have."

Joni was looking at him. There was no avoiding her accusation.

"I let her down?" he repeated. "Joni, I didn't do this on purpose."

"This is just like you," she said. "You've got a good heart, Terry, but you don't weigh your actions. You don't think about how anyone else might feel."

"I can't be responsible for other people." How many times had he said that in his life? Why did his words suddenly sound so selfish?

"I don't think Karen wants you to take responsibility for her." Joni nibbled at a tomato wedge. "I think she wants you to take responsibility for yourself."

"I do!"

"Asking her to risk her children's college money? Asking her to make you a loan?"

"With the house as security!"

"She sold the house because she couldn't afford to maintain it," Joni pointed out. "What kind of security is that?"

Terry stared glumly at his Happy Meal. Images kaleidoscoped through his memory: building a castle with Bopper, nestling a chinchilla in Rose's hands, climbing through the drainage ditch with Karen. He'd been playing as if he were a child, but he wasn't.

He didn't deserve a wife and children any more than Bobby did. The comparison hurt.

"What do you think I should do?" he asked.

"Find a way to qualify for a bank loan."

"Maybe I will," he said. "Thanks, Joni."

"It isn't the end of the world." She patted the back of his hand.

He supposed she was right.

WHAT REALLY MADE UP Terry's mind, in the end, was the phone call from Karen.

Brimming with cheer, she told him about her new job. "It's going to be a lot of work whipping things into shape, but I can use the challenge. It's the kind of experience I need.''

"Great."

"I'm going to go splurge on some little gifts for the kids," Karen said. "I've been tough on them the last few days. I'll see you at dinner."

"Right."

He hung up feeling deflated, even though he was pleased for Karen.

She'd marched out there and landed another job. She hadn't sobbed on a friend's shoulder. She hadn't sat around feeling sorry for herself.

Terry picked up the phone and called Lou Loomis at the ad agency.

FROM THEIR CORNER BOOTH at the crowded Sizzler restaurant, Karen watched Rose shepherd Bopper and Lisa through the dessert bar. How could one little boy pile so much chocolate pudding on a plate? How could he hope to eat it all after the swathe he'd cut through taco salad, spaghetti and the world's largest salad?

She'd arrived home to find Terry gone. At first, Karen thought it was strange he hadn't left a note. Then, with a pang, it occurred to her that Terry thought of himself as a roommate. If he wasn't a member of the family, there was no reason for him to account for his whereabouts.

That didn't have to stop her from celebrating her new job. She invited Marian and Lisa to be her guests for dinner. Since Sid was out of town, they'd been delighted.

"Karen?" Marian's soft voice cut through her thoughts. "While the kids are out of earshot...I think I might be pregnant."

"Marian!" Delight washed away Karen's concerns. "Oh, I'm so glad for you!"

"I don't want to tell anyone except you and Sid," her sister-in-law said. "I'm only five weeks along. Something might go wrong."

"Don't be such a pessimist!" But Karen understood. "I promise not to tell."

"I hate to get my hopes up," Marian admitted. "I want this baby so much."

The children trooped up with their desserts, halting the conversation. Watching Marian tuck a napkin around Lisa, Karen felt tears prick her eyes.

For all the problems with money, there was nothing more important than their families.

Another niece or nephew! She couldn't wait to gaze into a new pair of bright eyes, to watch a brand-new little person bloom through the stages of childhood.

The conversation shifted to Sid and Marian's seventh anniversary, which would occur Memorial Weekend. Karen insisted on hosting a family dinner.

"I want to hold it at our house," she said. "Once we move, we probably won't have room for everyone."

Bopper didn't notice, but Rose looked up, her lower lip caught in her teeth. Karen wanted to reassure her, but how could she? The new job meant they didn't have to pinch pennies, but it wouldn't cover buying back the house.

"Thanks," Marian said. "I'll bring dessert."

"No." Karen made a face at her. "It's your anniversary. For once, take it easy." To stave off an argument, she added, "Mom can bring the dessert."

They both liked that idea.

KAREN HAD FINISHED putting the children to bed when she heard Terry come home. She was surprised that he didn't call out.

She busied herself straightening the bathroom, but he didn't come upstairs. She went to give Rose another kiss and found the little girl already drifting off.

Karen smiled, seeing the childish face soften with sleep. Rose looked like a baby.

She peeked into Bopper's room and saw that he was absorbed in telling himself a story, so she tiptoed away.

At the head of the stairs, overlooking the front hall, Karen stood listening to the house as she had so many times these past few years since Bobby had left. Hearing the creaks and the silences, feeling the darkness descend beyond the windows. Knowing she and this house stood against wind and rain and night, protecting the children.

But Terry had become one of the guardians, too.

Alone here, attuned to the rustling sounds as he moved in the kitchen below, Karen let herself face what she'd been avoiding.

She'd fallen in love with Terry, more deeply than she'd realized. She couldn't shield herself from the pain if they parted. With Bobby, love had had years to fade before he actually left. Terry was different. Terry was someone she couldn't lose.

Even from this distance, she could feel his sadness. Unlike Bobby, Terry had a keen sense of letting them down, she knew. She'd seen it all weekend in his tensed jaw and hunched shoulders.

They would work this out together.

She slipped through the dark house into a pool of light bathing the kitchen. Her gaze traveled from the half-empty box of doughnuts on the table to a Terry she'd never seen before.

He wore a dark blue jacket over gray pants, a rumpled maroon tie striped with blue and gray, and a white button-down shirt.

As Terry held out the doughnut box wordlessly, Karen noticed details that had escaped her before. A defiant silver hair bristling at one of his temples. Faint lines tracing his mouth.

"I got a job, too," he said.

Karen edged onto a chair. "You did? How?"

"I called Lou, at the agency where I used to work. They just signed a new corporate client and they needed a copywriter."

"Oh, Terry." She didn't know how to respond. "I'm glad—I mean—"

He gave her a ghost of a smile. "They really liked my work and Lou gave me a top-notch recommendation."

"But your novel," she said.

"I'm stuck, anyway." He shrugged. "It won't kill me to go back to work. I've got until December to qualify for a loan. Once I've been on the job a few months, I'll start applying."

"Terry." Karen nibbled on some crumbs from the bottom of the doughnut box. "Are you sure this is what you want?"

"I want to be with you and the kids," he said. "Yes, I'm sure."

His eyes locked into hers. In their blue depths she saw flecks of aqua. Hints of another Terry, a man in place of a boy.

"You in a mood to celebrate?" she asked.

A low chuckle was response. "Doughnuts aren't enough?"

Karen poked him under the table. "Want to find out?"

They walked upstairs together.

Terry had changed, Karen found. He made love more slowly, watching as if seeing her for the first time. At first she felt self-conscious, but there was no mistaking the tenderness in his gaze.

By the time Terry entered her, Karen had forgotten everything but him. This time there were no fantasies about stars or oceans or mermaids' pools. There was only this man, lifting her into new sensations.

Chapter Fifteen

Every spring the Whittier Boomers sponsored a visit by the Easter Bunny and an egg hunt in a park behind the office.

Karen wasn't surprised that organizing the event turned out to be one of her duties. It fell more into the category of public relations than office management, but she wasn't going to quibble.

Setting up the event helped her feel that she was really part of the organization. It also provided a chance to see her four staffers in action and evaluate how they took responsibility outside their normal routine.

From the first day, she'd begun to assess their strengths and weaknesses. Tiffany, the receptionist, was punctual but needed to work on her professionalism. Nina, the senior member of the staff, took pride in her work but wasn't very flexible.

Joellen, in her early twenties, kept bankers' hours. Karen liked her high spirits, though.

Her biggest problem was Nancy. Proficient on the computer and knowledgeable about real estate, she clearly resented losing the promotion to Karen.

Nancy had made her own enemies by giving her favorite agents special treatment. She steered referrals from out-of-area agencies to her pals. This practice had caused considerable friction, and at least one agent had left the office because of it.

Of the four, only Nancy had failed to enter into the spirit of the Easter festivities. She made no secret of her disdain for the tradition.

By early Saturday morning, the day of the event, the eggs had been dyed—mostly by Karen and Nina—and the costumed bunny was flopping around the office while the photographer set up. Tiffany staffed the front desk as usual. People wanted to buy and sell houses even on Easter weekend.

"This looks great." Beverly Blankenship walked outside with Karen to survey the streamers and balloons festooning the park.

Karen checked her watch. A quarter to nine. "People should be here soon."

A car door slammed, and Nina hurried toward them. "Can you believe I ran out of Scotch tape?" The woman set an armload of wrapped packages—prizes for the children who found special eggs—onto a covered picnic table.

"They look beautiful." Karen fingered the colorful wrappings.

"I've got to finish these. I'll just run inside." Nina departed and returned in a flash.

Across the park, Karen spotted Joellen, in a clown costume, waving to families as they approached. The receptionist handed each child a balloon printed with the name of the real-estate firm.

"You've done a good job," Beverly told Karen. "My last office manager took this on like Hercules cleaning the Augean stables—pinching her nose. You seem to enjoy it."

"Must be because I have kids. I'm glad we can do something for the community." Karen checked out the parking lot. "Has anyone seen Nancy?"

The broker shook her head.

Nancy had grumbled about having to work on a Saturday, but all the staff members had been offered a choice of overtime or a compensatory day off. "I'm sure she'll be here," Nina said. "She knows we need her to line up the kids for photographs."

Karen hurried inside, but there was no sign of the missing staffer. Parents and children milled around the outer office, while Tiffany gestured helplessly from where she sat juggling nonstop phone calls.

The front door opened, and with a rush of relief Karen spotted Terry, followed by Marian and the children.

"Oh, please!" Karen cried. "Terry, help!"

He went to work with good cheer, steering the families one at a time to the bunny in Beverly's sanctum. Marian took Rose, Bopper and Lisa to the egg hunt.

Karen took a moment to watch Terry. He was kneeling next to a toddler, patiently repeating the words "Bunny!" and "Picture!" and "Candy!"

How thoughtful he was. Even as she appreciated his gentleness, she wondered why she missed the Terry who bounded about like Tigger, blew soap bubbles and led Christmas carols on the porch.

For the next few hours, she shuttled back and forth between office and park, making sure everything went off as planned. Nina did an excellent job of marshaling the hunt, and Joellen clowned and romped to everyone's delight.

Nancy arrived two hours late, in company with Maureen, one of the top agents. "She needed help with a listing presentation," Nancy announced. She went directly into Maureen's office and began typing.

Karen took a couple of deep breaths. This was not the time for a confrontation. She would need to prepare before she tackled Nancy head-on.

Beverly Blankenship had noticed the staffer's behavior and didn't look pleased. That was a good sign, Karen told herself as Nancy strode through the lobby to the ladies' room, wearing an expression of haughty exasperation.

"Do I sense an office prima donna?" Terry murmured.

She grimaced. "My problem child."

"Sic 'em," he muttered. She grinned.

They stood side by side, handing out candy and directing youngsters to the bunny. To other people, Terry probably looked relaxed, but Karen noticed the stiffness in his shoulders and the tense angle of his chin. She realized with a start that he'd been this way for the past several weeks, since he had begun his job.

Nancy emerged from the ladies' room. Karen blocked her path. "Take over here," she snapped, and led Terry outside.

"That was not a happy camper," he reported as they hurried toward the park. "Either she was grimacing at you or there's gargoyle blood in her veins."

"Both," Karen said. She stopped, her hand on Terry's arm. "What—"

A red-haired man was helping Rose lift her egg-filled basket onto a table for counting. Behind him, Bopper hopped up and down, heedless of the damage to his own eggs.

Bobby. He must have read about the egg hunt in the paper and seen Karen's name.

Before she could decide what to do, Marian joined them. "He brought some eggs he'd decorated himself," she said. "Nina asked him to hide them so all the kids would have an equal chance, and he did."

"He hasn't ruined anything yet?"

Marian chuckled. "No."

Bopper seemed happy enough and even Rose was chattering with her father. Then, catching sight of Karen, the little girl paused as if awaiting a signal.

Old memories pinched Karen—Bobby's heedless departure, the smashed Christmas ornaments, the children's tears. All part of the past. Time to let go.

"I guess the kids need their father." She forced herself to smile and wave at Rose. "In small doses."

Terry squeezed her arm. "It can't be easy," he said. "But you're right."

"He really misses them, in his own way," Marian said. "And they miss him. He'll never be the kind of father they need day-to-day, but some contact will be good for all of them."

The biggest surprise came a short time later, while the children were filling up on candy, raisins and nuts. Bobby slipped a check into Karen's hand.

It was for a hundred dollars. Only a token, after two years, but to him it represented a lot.

"I got this job in an art-supply store." He shifted from foot to foot. "In Pasadena. Thought I could help out a little, if you'll let me visit the kids."

"Okay," Karen said. "Be sure to call first."

Bobby nodded, avoiding her gaze. "Yeah. Well, I better be hitting the freeway."

He kissed Bopper and Rose on his way out. Busy eating, they scarcely noticed. Bobby walked on, his shoulders drooping.

"If he knew them better, he'd understand," Terry said.

"Kids don't always look past the moment," Karen agreed.

"I think Bobby's beginning to understand the price he's paid for his selfishness." Marian folded her arms across her abdomen.

The gesture reminded Karen of her sister-in-law's pregnancy. She assumed all was going well. She decided not to ask—Marian would bring it up when she felt like discussing it.

Instead, she hugged her friend. "I love you."

Marian blinked. "What brought that on?"

"Do I need an excuse?"

Her sister-in-law smiled. "I love you, too, Karen."

"Can anyone play?" asked Terry. "I love you both."

"Equally?" Karen teased.

"I'd have to taste more of Marian's cooking before I could answer that."

She gave him a playful punch.

"HOW ABOUT, 'Caresses your legs, all the way up?'" Terry tried not to blanch as he spoke. He wondered how the account executive and the creative director could sit there nodding gravely while listening to such beeswax.

"I'm not sure if a feminine audience would have the right reaction to that." Melina, a whiz at synthesizing ideas, who had been promoted to creative director at the age of twenty-eight, studied the pair of panty hose dangling over the back of a chair.

Roy, the account executive, a trim man in his forties whose skin had been tanned the color of old leather, reached to stroke the stockings. It had been his idea to hang them there in the first place, for inspiration.

This was their first ad campaign for Magic Legs, and they needed a winner.

Terry supposed a panty hose manufacturer must be an ideal client. Come hell or high water, women still needed stockings, thanks to snags and runs. He couldn't tell the difference between one brand and another. He assumed the makers relied on advertising to sell the sizzle.

The problem was, he had trouble getting enthusiastic about nylons. Taking the stockings off... There was something a man could contemplate with real interest.

"How about, 'You put 'em on, he'll take 'em off,'" he suggested.

"Too blunt." Melina frowned at the notes she was taking.

"I like the sexuality angle," Roy said. "If we can tone it down."

"They're priced at the low end—a good buy." Melina looked as if she were drawing arrows on her notes, connecting thoughts.

"We'll give you a run for your money!" Terry quipped. The others laughed.

Silence fell as they contemplated the panty hose. It dominated the conference room. Which wasn't difficult, Terry reflected.

Terry knew there must still be a world outside, in which panty hose was simply a utilitarian object that women tossed into the shopping cart. A world in which the decision to buy Magic Legs was made not because of overwhelming lust but because an old pair of hose had disintegrated beyond the point where clear nail polish could rescue it.

He wondered if he would ever see that world again.

"We've got to come up with something," Roy said. "We're up against a deadline here."

"Makes you feel like dancing," Terry threw out.

"Been done."

"Gentlemen prefer... Nope, that's Hanes."

"Let's play on the word 'feelings,'" Melina said. "Silky feelings."

"Feel silky!" Terry offered.

Roy took out a cigarette and twiddled it. Smoking wasn't allowed outside the lunchroom, but he needed a prop. "Feel silky! Feel sexy!"

"You're hitting them over the head." Melina flipped a page in her notebook.

"Feel silky. Feel sensuous," Terry said.

"Good, good!" Melina tapped her pen against the paper to get the ink flowing. "One more adjective. A trilogy. Like—confident. Feel silky, feel sensuous, feel sure of yourself?"

"Feel silky, feel sensuous, feel self-assured." Roy was good at wining-and-dining clients, but he had no poetry in his soul.

"Serene," said Terry.

"That's it!" Melina crowed. "Feel silky, feel sensuous, feel serene!"

An echo mocked through Terry's mind. *Feel silly, feel stupid, feel like you sold out.*

"Congratulations, Terry." Roy shook his hand. "Terrific!"

"Glad we've got you on board." Melina stood up and pumped his hand.

"Thanks." Terry kept a bland expression on his face as they preceded him from the room.

He strolled back to his office, relieved that the slogan had passed muster. He had nothing to do the rest of the day but look busy. Advertising personified the old army saying, hurry up and wait. In this case, though, it was more like, wait and hurry up.

He might have nothing to do for days, and then—usually on a Friday afternoon, like today—someone would toss him a rush job.

Terry had tried using spare time to work on his book, but the ideas wouldn't come. Only a hundred pages remained, but he lacked both the enthusiasm and the right twist for the climax.

Hard to believe he'd been working here two months. It was already Memorial Weekend. The start of summer. As if you could track the seasons, in this tinted, air-conditioned office.

He popped into the lunchroom and faced a high-tech array of vending machines.

The sound of voices drew his attention toward the doorway as Lou Loomis appeared with a Japanese businessman. Terry remembered hearing mention of a potential new client, a video-game manufacturer.

He wouldn't mind working on that account if it came with free samples.

"This is our lunchroom, Mr. Fujita," Lou said. "That's Terry Vogel, our resident author."

"Terry Vogel!" Mr. Fujita's face lit up. "*Major League Vampire,* yes?"

Terry nodded, surprised. The book had been translated into Japanese, but it hadn't occurred to him anyone had actually read it.

"Very fine!" Mr. Fujita hurried to shake his hand. "You work here?"

"I'm a copywriter," Terry said.

"You will work on my account?"

Terry glanced at Lou to make sure he wasn't stepping on any toes, then said, "Sure."

"Very good." Mr. Fujita nodded as if he'd just concluded a deal. "Terry Vogel!" He rejoined Lou, but looked back before departing. "Next book, I need autographed copies."

"Sure thing."

Terry selected a root beer and retrieved the can.

Mr. Fujita's admiration bothered him. Paradoxically, the praise reminded Terry that right now he wasn't much of an author. He'd hit a case of writer's block that might be permanent.

It was his own fault, for being overly optimistic about reaching the big time. He'd set himself up to fail.

Terry paced to his cubbyhole of an office, propped his legs on the desk and stared at the computer screen. Only an hour until he could hit the freeway. That would be something less than fun on the eve of a holiday weekend. He didn't look forward to watching the temperature needle edge toward meltdown as he sat in a traffic jam.

Then he remembered. He wouldn't be driving the dragon, with its temperamental cooling system.

This morning, he'd bought a new car. It wasn't actually new—he'd found a good deal on an Audi that one of the executives wanted to trade in.

It drove without chugging and no springs protruded from the seats. Besides, the dragon had begun attracting too much interest from unsavory characters in the parking garage.

On his lunch hour, he'd donated the dragon to a children's hospital, which would use it for fund-raising events.

Terry had debated spending money on the Audi, but it wasn't enough to make a difference on the house. Besides, with his current salary, plus bonuses, he'd have no trouble qualifying for a loan.

He wondered if he would still feel like the same person, driving a conventional car. He'd miss the cheerful waves of onlookers, the children's faces pressed against their car windows as they stared at him.

The circus wouldn't be coming to town anymore.

Good. He didn't want to fight his new role. He wanted to be the kind of man Karen and the children needed.

The wall clock clicked toward quitting time. Terry hooded his computer and strode out.

Karen hadn't mentioned his offer of marriage again. She probably wondered how long he could go on like this.

The children would be spending the evening at Marian's, while Karen prepared for tomorrow's anniversary dinner. It meant a chance to catch her alone for an intimate talk.

He intended to make her see that he really had changed, forever.

KAREN HAD HOPED to make an early getaway from the office, to get a head start on cleaning the house and shopping for groceries.

At the front desk, Tiffany and Joellen applied themselves to the busy phones. After several infractions, Joellen had cleaned up her act and would soon be off probation.

Playing disciplinarian wasn't Karen's first choice. It came with the territory.

It didn't bother her to contemplate leaving early herself. She'd put in plenty of extra hours.

On her way to fetch her purse, Karen checked Beverly's office. Empty. The broker hadn't stuck around, either.

"Karen?" It was John Garcia, one of the up-and-coming agents. "You seen Bev?"

"I guess she's gone." Karen forced herself not to fidget. "Anything I can help you with?"

"It's Nancy." He clenched his teeth as if considering biting someone. "There's a serious problem."

"Let's talk about it." Karen waited.

A phone call had come in, he said, from a resident of John's "farm," a neighborhood where he solicited business door-to-door and distributed fliers. Although other agents from the office could take listings there, they couldn't knock on doors or advertise directly.

The caller, who wanted to sell his house, had seen one of John's signs, but didn't remember his name and simply asked to speak to an agent.

Nancy, although knowing that the client lived in John's farm, had referred the call to Maureen, who had taken the listing.

"That's my territory," John said. "I work hard there, and he called because of my sign. Nancy knew the call should have gone to me."

"I'll speak to her—"

"That isn't enough! I've had it with her. She just ripped me off for thousands of dollars, and this isn't the first time. Some of the other agents are up in arms, too."

She couldn't leave this issue hanging over the long weekend. John deserved justice.

"You're right," she said. "I'll lay down the law. If she pulls anything like this again, she's fired."

"You ought to fire her now!" He paced along the hall. "I know you walked into the middle of this, Karen, but—"

"It's my job," she finished. "I should have confronted her before. I can't fire her without a proper warning. But she'd better find a new attitude and quick."

He nodded. "Thanks, Karen. Sorry to dump this on you right before a holiday."

"I'll take care of it."

She found Nancy in the snack room. The secretary insisted she was about to depart and didn't have time to talk. Karen told her in a low voice that they had to speak now.

Nancy gave in with poor grace.

When they were both inside her office, Karen offered Nancy a chair. She refused and stood with hands on hips, glaring out the window.

"You gave an up-call from John's farm to Maureen," Karen said. "That's a violation of policy."

"He wasn't around." Nancy shrugged.

"Then you should have taken a message."

"And risk losing the client? What if they called another agency?" Nancy sneered. "If you'd been around here longer, you'd understand these things."

"What the client chooses to do isn't your problem," Karen said. "You could have paged John. You could have asked Beverly to handle it."

"I don't need you to tell me my job." Nancy's cheeks reddened. "You parade around like you were some kind of royalty. Well, you're not my boss. Beverly is. Let her tell me herself, if she wants to."

"You're fired," Karen said. "Collect your things. You've got two weeks' severance pay, but I don't want to see you around here."

"You can't fire me! It isn't up to you!"

"You didn't read my job description," Karen said.

"Wait till Maureen hears about this!" Nancy was shouting now, loud enough to be heard throughout the building. Karen hoped all the agents had gone home, but she doubted it.

"Maureen is free to hire you herself," Karen said, although she couldn't imagine anything she'd like less than seeing Nancy's face around the office again. She hoped Maureen was too cheap to pay a full-time assistant.

"I'm not leaving!" The shriek rang out so loud Karen almost didn't hear her door opening.

"Yes, you are."

They both turned to see Beverly. She hadn't left for the day, after all.

"She—" Nancy began.

"I heard about it from John," the broker said. "I already lost one agent because of you, Nancy. I should have fired you then. Karen does have the authority and she's simply saved me the trouble. Out."

Nancy shoved her way out the door and stomped off.

Karen shook her head. "I hate to do this. We can't even give her a recommendation."

"I'm sure Maureen will do that." Beverly shrugged. "We've done her a favor. Nancy was poisoning herself with resentment. Now she can look for a job that suits her."

"If I'd known you were coming back—"

"You handled this fine." The broker smiled. "I think you're going to be around a lot longer than six months. Now why don't you go enjoy your holiday?"

Not until she'd reached her car did Karen discover she was trembling from a combination of relief and delayed shock.

Karen thought back to her class, to the presentations she'd made and the satisfaction of receiving an *A*. What she hadn't realized was that the real test had been still to come.

Today, she'd taken it. And passed.

She gave herself a mental pat on the back and felt her spirits lift.

Her thoughts turned to Terry's proposal. He must be expecting an answer soon. Karen wasn't sure why she kept procrastinating.

Was it fear that he might change his mind? Or a sense that something had vanished from their relationship?

She spotted the Audi in front of the house as she pulled into the driveway and wondered who it belonged to. A glance at the dashboard clock told her Terry should be home by now, even with freeway traffic, but she didn't see his dragon.

Karen walked over to the Audi. On the bumper she spotted a parking sticker from the ad agency.

The dragon would prowl no more.

A sharp sense of loss pricked at her. That dragon had been childish and magical, immature and daring, impractical and bold. Now it was gone.

And she wanted it back.

Chapter Sixteen

"But the new car isn't you." Karen ducked into the downstairs bathroom to change into jeans.

"It is now."

She'd found Terry reorganizing the videotapes in the den, bringing some of the children's forgotten treasures to the front. She gathered he was looking forward to watching the tapes himself.

This Karen took as a good sign that he hadn't entirely lost his playful side, but he wouldn't budge on the car. Terry wouldn't even tell her what he'd done with the old one.

"You'd just go down and commiserate with it," he said.

"Don't be silly." Karen emerged and searched under the stairs for her jogging shoes. "Have you thought what the kids are going to say?"

"They'll get over it." He tossed her the shoes from the dining room. Karen remembered now that Bopper had been parading around in them this morning.

"I'm off." She retrieved her grocery list from the kitchen.

"Want a test drive? I'll take you to the store."

"How could I refuse?"

She had to admit the ride was smooth. No more jouncing over every bump or swaying dangerously on sharp turns.

No more laughs and cheers from bystanders, either.

"I miss the old car and I miss the old you," she said.

"Yes, but you're the woman who once married Bobby," Terry reminded her. "Your judgment isn't entirely reliable."

She smacked him with her grocery list.

They walked side by side into a glaringly bright supermarket. Whatever spirit ruled grocery stores in Southern California must have decided a few years earlier that it was time to redecorate. One by one, all the stores in Karen's neighborhood had been ripped apart and stuffed with intense lighting, curved refrigerator sections, display islands and such trendy decorator colors as mauve and aqua.

"I can't find anything anymore," she grumbled, pushing a recalcitrant cart down the aisle.

Terry pointed to a computer screen. "Type in what you're looking for and *presto magico.*"

"They should have left things where they were. I make up my grocery list in order, and now I've got to start all over again memorizing their layout." Karen didn't know what had put her in such a grouchy mood.

It wasn't hard to figure out, though. Too many things were changing too fast. Her job. The supermarket. Terry's car.

Terry.

"You really want the dragon back?" he asked as she selected two cans of cranberry sauce.

"No. I want you back." She grabbed a can of pineapple chunks. "Doggone it. Where's the apple juice?"

Terry checked a list he'd mysteriously acquired. "Aisle seven. You want me back? Here I am."

"I want the old, crazy Terry," Karen admitted. "I want to have fun. I want a man who acts like an idiot."

"I always thought there was something strange about you." He located a box of brown sugar on the bottom shelf. "Isn't this on your list?"

"You read it before I got home!"

"Making sure you weren't going to poison us with one of those low-fat, no-cholesterol deals. I'm happy to say I like glazed ham, sweet potatoes, cauliflower and a green salad, if it's not too green."

"Terry," she said. "I'm serious."

"The old Terry couldn't get a loan."

He had a point. Karen didn't know what had gotten into her tonight.

The departure of the dragon V-Dub, she realized, marked a permanent change. Subconsciously, she'd been expecting him to snap back to his old self after a while.

"I guess what I miss—" she tossed in two cans of sweet potatoes "—is the way we used to play."

"We haven't had a lot of fun these past six weeks," he agreed.

"It's as if a light's gone out." She hated facing the truth. "I feel as if I pinned down a butterfly and it faded in front of my eyes. You're not the same, Terry."

"I can't deny it." He sighed. "I've been hit by a writer's block so big I think they made it out of the old Berlin Wall."

Their eyes met over the shopping cart. "I can't ask you to live this way." Karen gripped the handle to keep from trembling. "Maybe we're not right for each other, Terry."

"We have to be," he said. "I love you."

A gray-haired woman paused nearby examining two different styles of canned cherries, one in each hand.

"Sometimes love isn't..." Karen refused to finish the cliché.

"...enough," the woman prompted.

"Thank you." Terry bowed.

Karen pulled him into another aisle. "What I'm trying to say is, life has a way of throwing in a monkey wrench. Terry, you can't tell me you're happy at your job."

"I'm happy at my job," he said.

"You're lying!"

"Well, yes."

"I can't take it. You've gone all gray inside. You stand there every morning knotting your tie and hating it." She stopped by a display of canned hams.

"Can't a man have any privacy? You analyze how I tie my tie?" He picked up a ham and read the label. "You don't want this one. It's made out of a pig."

"Put that back." She selected a different one. "You're a menace in the supermarket."

"It's my only creative outlet." He trailed alongside her. "Karen, relationships go through phases. Right now we're in a period of building. It's supposed to be stressful."

She stared at him. "You never used to say things like that."

"I heard it on the radio, driving to work."

She had to laugh. That *did* sound like the old Terry. "You'll say anything if it sounds good, won't you?"

He fell silent as they cruised the dairy section. Karen managed to sneak a carton of nonfat sour cream substitute and a gallon of extra-light milk into the cart without his noticing.

They had reached the detergent aisle, and she was debating between cleanser with bleach or without when Terry spoke again.

"At first I was just playing a role," he said. "The man in the gray flannel suit. But I've been thinking about a lot of things. Being in my thirties. Needing to help support a family."

"Everybody goes through that," Karen said.

"It's all tied in with my writer's block." Terry frowned at the teddy bear on a bottle of fabric softener, as if offended by its manipulative cuteness. "I've been thinking that maybe it's time I wrote something serious. In the horror field, perhaps, but not so flippant."

Something was very, very wrong. Not with what he was saying, but with his body language. In the bright, flat lighting, the muscles in his face had tightened, shifting all the planes so he looked like a different person.

"You're wrong," Karen said. "You need to loosen up."

He folded his arms. "You have a history of liking men who are boyish and—let's face it—irresponsible. Maybe you're having a hard time letting go of that, Karen."

His perceptiveness startled her. She thought of her mother and how unprepared she'd been when Helene learned to drive. Karen had played the same role since adolescence, always the strong one, always the adult.

"Possibly. I'll give it some thought." Well, they wouldn't find any answers here, shelved between the spray starch and the stain sticks.

They trailed into the produce department. Terry helped round up the salad makings and cauliflower. He was nestling a bag of tomatoes into the cart when he stopped dead, staring at a point over Karen's shoulder.

"Oh, no," he said.

Above the fresh juice section hung a sign—"Eat fresh! Feel fresh!"

"Not more slogans!" Terry muttered. "Big Brother is watching you. 'Eat fresh! Feel fresh!' What are we supposed to do, smear guava juice under our armpits?"

"Terry!" Karen poked him.

"Eat fresh! Feel fresh!" His voice rose. Other shoppers glanced up. "It's the thought police. Careful! The rutabagas are watching. Do we have to maintain the proper healthful attitude at all times? Can't we just buy vegetables?"

Karen checked her list. "I think we're done."

Terry snatched up a pineapple by its spiky crown. "You! Have you filed your report yet? Are we eating fresh enough?"

A thin, balding man stopped sniffing a cantaloupe and chuckled.

"I hate this crap," Terry said. "Why do we have to feel fresh? People don't cook dinner anymore, they get masters' degrees in nutrition. Laser guns from the planet Lard-o zap you, if you inject any actual taste."

"Haven't you seen the latest recommendations from the USDA?" It was the lady with the cherry cans, which were now wedged beneath a flowery head of kale. "You know, young man, you really should think of your health."

"I am thinking of my health!" Terry said. "My mental health!"

Karen steered him toward the checkout line.

"We're being overrun by oat bran! Terrorized by tofu!" He clapped groceries onto the conveyer.

"Is he all right?" the checker asked.

"He just needs a vacation." Karen handed over her coupons.

"That's what you think." Terry plopped a head of lettuce onto the belt. "We're being bombarded by broccoflower and strafed by strawberries."

Karen wrote a check. "Good thing it's a three-day weekend."

"I know what you mean," said the checker.

"I will not eat fresh!" Terry said.

A bearded man, celery and carrots peeping from his paper sack, nodded as he walked by. "I'm with you, man. Eat low on the food chain."

"I said fresh, not flesh!" Terry had the grace to look embarrassed at the man's startled reaction.

"Are you done?" Karen helped the checker fill up their sacks.

"I suppose," he said. "Yes, okay. I'm done."

"Something snapped, didn't it?" she asked as he wheeled the cart out.

Terry nodded glumly.

"All that stuff about how you've changed, you were just trying to convince yourself, weren't you?"

He let out a long sigh that seemed to come from all the way down in his socks.

"Quit your job," she said.

"No." He opened the trunk and plunked in a sack. "It's not that bad, Karen."

"You're selling your soul to the ad agency and I won't have it." She tossed in a bottle of cleanser. "I'll loan you the money from my savings and you can take as long as you need to pay me back. Okay?"

He stood with a sack suspended over the trunk, staring into the twilit sky.

"Terry?"

He set down the sack.

"Terry?" Karen repeated.

"Yeah." It wasn't really an answer.

Puzzled, she kept silent as they got into the car. Terry didn't speak, not even when they'd exited the parking lot and were heading home.

"Did I say something wrong?" Karen asked.

"Mmm-mmm." It sounded like a negative. But if she hadn't said anything wrong, why had he cut her off like this?

She'd thought she knew Terry in all his moods, but not this one. He didn't seem to be sulking as he drove— he'd simply tuned her out.

As if she no longer mattered.

Karen tried to replay their interaction. Was he angry that she'd chided him in front of the checker? Had he expected to draw a more appreciative audience with his outburst?

Those were the kinds of triggers that might have set Bobby off. But not Terry.

Still locked in his own thoughts when they reached home, he unloaded the groceries in a zombie-like state. When everything was put away, he walked upstairs without a word.

Karen heard the rowing machine start up. The rhythmic thumping told her more about the turbulence in Terry's mind than any speech could have.

Sometimes love isn't enough.

They couldn't work things out, if he wouldn't talk to her. Uneasily Karen left to fetch the children, without calling up to say goodbye.

He wouldn't hear her over the machine. Even if he did, she knew by now that he wouldn't respond.

TERRY STAYED IN his room most of Saturday, although Karen didn't hear the rowing machine any more. He came downstairs about ten in the morning to snatch a box of crackers and a block of cheese, along with some mismatched cans of soda.

He kissed the tops of the children's heads and disappeared again.

"Is he mad at us?" Bopper asked.

"Not at you." It was midafternoon, and Karen had begun preparing dinner.

It was hard to believe Sid and Marian had been married seven years. Cleaning the cauliflower, Karen thought back to their wedding at a jewel of a church in Long Beach.

She remembered standing by the altar, as matron of honor, watching Marian march up the aisle with her uncle. The bride's smile gleamed right through the veil.

Karen's brother waited by the minister. Rough-and-tumble Sid, whom she'd hardly ever seen out of jeans and a work shirt, angled his neck as if trying to escape the confines of the bow tie.

A ray of sunlight caught him as he focused on Marian. His expression softened with love and pride. In that moment he seemed aglow. Then his bride moved into the sunlight with him, sharing the shining circle.

Karen couldn't recall what the minister had said, what traditional phrases he had recited or what personal wisdom he might have imparted. She was left with the impression of having witnessed a spiritual union that transcended anything man could put together or take apart.

That, she knew, was the way marriage was supposed to be. She was glad her brother had found it. She wondered if she ever would.

In the restless hours the previous night, when sleep hadn't come, Karen had realized what might be troubling Terry.

She'd offered to loan him the money, but she'd never mentioned his proposal of marriage. She'd spoken of "I" and "you," not "we."

She'd encouraged him to quit his job, but she'd made it clear that when he did she would still hold the reins of power. He was right. She hadn't been willing to let go of her role as the adult and join him on an equal basis.

It was enough to make anyone angry. But did he have to punish her with silence? It came between them like an ever-widening gap.

FOR ONCE, MARIAN didn't sense that something was afoot. No wonder. She'd taken the plunge, abandoning her disguising muumuus for a down-and-out maternity dress.

"Nine weeks," she declared as she hugged Karen. "I'm finally letting myself believe this little guy's going to be okay."

"I never thought of you as a worrywart." Karen gave her brother a kiss, too.

"She has this idea it's bad luck to take things for granted." Sid shook his head. "I think taking things for granted is half the fun in life."

They didn't seem to notice Terry's absence even after they'd sent Lisa off to play with her cousins and settled around the living room. The baby-to-be-was too all-absorbing.

"I haven't told Helene yet," Marian admitted. "She's been so busy since she got back from her honeymoon."

With a guilty twinge, Karen realized she hadn't had more than a few brief phone conversations with her mother this past month.

Helene and Frederick seemed to live in a whirlwind. Whenever Karen talked to them, they were off to an art museum or a play or busy with volunteer work. They'd both taken a class in teaching literacy and were spending several afternoons a week tutoring adult nonreaders.

"I feel as if I've neglected them," Karen said.

"You've been busy." Marian smiled. "Me, too. I'd forgotten about all those doctor visits. And the morning sickness. It's miserable, but it's worth it." She looked around. "Say, where's Terry?"

Karen didn't know how to explain. She was beginning to feel irritated with Terry for putting her in this situation.

He knew about tonight's dinner. Was he planning to spoil it for everyone?

As she searched for an answer, the doorbell rang.

Helene and Frederick stood outside with their arms entwined. They released each other reluctantly to shake hands and share hugs, and then Helene noticed the maternity dress.

The air shimmered with phrases like "due at Christmas" and "positively radiant" and "we think maybe Joshua, if it's a boy, or Esther, if it's a girl."

They were setting out the food when Helene, too, noticed something amiss. "Isn't Terry here?"

"He's upstairs," Karen said. "I'm not sure what he's busy with."

"I'm sure it's something interesting." Marian set water glasses around the table. "Shall we seat the kids together or break them up?"

"As far apart as possible," Karen said.

Footsteps skittered down the stairs. Terry appeared in the dining room doorway, hair freshly washed and face bright. "How is everybody?"

The responses filled the air. Before Karen knew it, the children were racing in and she was too busy getting them settled and serving dinner to query further.

The ham, potatoes, cauliflower and salad disappeared in record time, and then Frederick raised his wineglass. "I propose a toast," he said. "To Sid and Marian."

Everyone cheered and drank, the children sipping at their juice.

Sid lifted his glass. "To Helene and Frederick!"

The others chorused their approval and drank.

Just when Karen thought the toasts were finished, Terry raised his hand. "One more," he said.

Uh-oh. Her hands crumpled the napkin in her lap.

"To Karen," Terry said. "Who has knocked down the Berlin Wall."

The family regarded him blankly.

"My monumental case of writer's block has been cured," Terry explained. "It was Karen who gave me the idea. She didn't want me to sell my soul to the ad agency. But what if someone did? What would an ad agency want with souls? Think of the commercials the devil would make if he had the chance! I've been up all night writing my outline. I'm calling it *The Demon in the Gray Flannel Suit*."

"You mean you're giving up on *Dream a Little Scream of Me?*" Marian asked.

"Oh, no. I've figured out how to finish that one, too. I'll whip it off in a few weekends, so I can get on with the good stuff." Terry rubbed his hands together. "Of course this means I'll have to stay on at the ad agency for a while. Doing research."

"You don't mind?" Karen said.

"We just landed a video-game account. I wouldn't miss that one for the world!"

After the toast, Helene remembered she'd left the cheesecake in her car, and the children trooped out with her to get it.

The wine must have gone to Karen's head, because she spent the rest of the evening in a blur. How could she have suspected Terry of underhanded behavior? Sulking had never been his style. Why hadn't it occurred to her that he was writing?

Maybe she loved him too much to be objective.

Helene and Frederick put Rose and Bopper to bed, and then it was time for goodbyes. Karen squeezed Marian's hand and whispered that she was looking forward to the family's Christmas present; Sid and Frederick clapped each other on the back. There were hugs all around, then suddenly the house was empty.

Almost empty.

Karen found Terry in the kitchen, humming as he washed the dishes.

"Tonight was fun." He looked so dear, standing there wearing an apron, a fleck of soapsuds on his cheek. "I don't suppose there's any cheesecake left, is there?"

"Not hardly. You ought to know. You only ate three pieces."

To Karen, at this moment, everything seemed so simple, like a tangled gold chain unknotting beneath a drop of oil. She couldn't tame the future and lock it in a cage. She had to carry it openhanded, holding it up to the sky.

"We do have one more thing to celebrate," she said.

Terry stopped drying a wineglass.

"It's the answer to your question," she said.

"I love riddles!" Terry chewed on his lip. "My question? Did I ask one?"

"Yes," she said.

"Does it have anything to do with food?"

"No."

"The children?"

"No."

"Give me another clue." He polished a plate.

"The answer to the question might be 'I will,' or maybe 'I do.'"

He didn't move. Didn't blink, didn't dry any dishes, didn't swallow.

"It's usually followed by a romantic declaration such as 'I love you,'" Karen prompted.

He dropped the dish towel, walked over and hugged her. "I love you."

She slid her hands over his muscular arms and pressed her cheek against his. He smelled of wine and lemon detergent with a hint of cheesecake.

"Let's dirty up some more glasses," Terry said. "This calls for another toast."

Karen shook her head. "My knees will give out."

"We need to do something. This is a pivotal moment in my life."

"The stars," she said.

They walked out to the back porch and sat on the swing. Pricks of light sparkled in the dark arch of the night. Karen relaxed against Terry's warmth, her leg tangling between his.

"There." She pointed to a bright point overhead. "That's our star."

"That's an AT&T satellite."

She poked him with her elbow. "Terry!"

"But I'm glad we have a star," he said. "Something we can dream on."

"Good. You haven't forgotten how to dream." An evening mist was beginning to creep across the sky, blurring reality with a magical softness.

"I never will," he said, "now that I have you."

They leaned back, staring upward. They stayed there for a long time, watching the lights in the sky, whatever they were.

Epilogue

When Gladys Maycap tapped her way into the hotel lobby, a cane in one hand and a carved stone bottle in the other, King Tut regarded her with knowing eyes.

The hotel was decorated in the style of the pharaohs. Mrs. Maycap had awakened this morning knowing that she must come. She stood before a vast atrium, a dozen stories high, dripping with plants like the Hanging Gardens of Babylon. Statues of Egyptian gods loomed above sunken pools.

A couple of Junior Achievers jostled past, on their way to join their fellow conventioneers. Rowdy children had no place in this temple, she reflected as she looked down at the small stone bottle she'd brought.

Gladys traced the leering face carved into it. She had loved this bottle since childhood, as it sat in its alcove in church. It had been brought back from North Africa fifty years earlier by a missionary who had believed it to be a holy relic.

Gladys knew better.

She had felt the thing calling. On her sixteenth birthday, Gladys stole it. It had ruled her life ever since.

Lately, dreams had told Gladys that she must free the Lord of Destruction.

And they must get rid of these children.

Terry stretched. He felt Karen slip into the room and pause behind his chair, but he didn't speak. He was on a roll.

Gladys Maycap lifted the bottle and called out the name of the god Tunkhara.

A gray cloud drifted through the lobby. The children's voices became muted. Movement slowed.

Gladys didn't notice the slim young woman look up from hanging venetian blinds in the hotel restaurant.

Bridget Weintraub felt an ancient chill and knew it had found her, the thing she had been tracking all these months.

Inside her purse her fingers closed on a tiny scarab.

Only this sacred beetle of the ancients could kill the thing forever.

As Bridget reached the doorway to the lobby, the beast struck. Scarlet heat snapping with black smoke pierced Bridget's throat.

Then she saw him. Herbert. The muscular man with the hooded eyes. He'd told her he was a Junior Achievers counselor. Now she knew he was the archaeologist whose scarab had been delivered to her by mistake, the man she was destined to meet.

He struggled toward her through the thick air, clutching a polished teak cross. A wall of fire leaped in front of Bridget. With her last sliver of strength, she flung the scarab toward Herbert.

Just before the darkness claimed her, she heard him call out. "Bridget! Bridget! My love!"

Terry saved the file in his computer. The actual destruction of the beast would take a few pages more to accomplish, but he felt satisfied. Not only would good triumph over evil, but Bridget was going to find true love as well.

Hands massaged his shoulders. "I like it," Karen said. "Is there really a hotel like that in Buffalo?"

"I doubt it." He grinned. "But there's one a few miles from here, in Brea. I borrowed it."

"Is that fair?"

"How would anyone know?" he said. "Unless you tell them."

"Not me." She gave him a hug. "I'll let you get on with your work."

"I'd rather play," he hinted, remembering that the children had gone out with their grandparents today.

She kissed the tip of his ear. "I know you're in a hurry to finish. Anyway, what I really need is an opinion. What do you think of lavender and white for our colors?"

She and her mother were planning the wedding at Karen's church, with the reception at the house.

"It sounds silky, sensuous and serene," Terry said.

She chuckled. "Remember that line when we're honeymooning in Honolulu."

"We won't need words. We'll be carried away by the sunlight and the ocean and the quicksilver flow of our blood." He drew her closer.

"I can't wait," she said.

Terry discovered that he couldn't, either.

HARLEQUIN
American Romance®

American Romance's year-long celebration continues. Join your favorite authors as they celebrate love set against the special times each month throughout 1992.

Next month, recall those sweet memories of summer love, of long, hot days...and even hotter nights in:

AUGUST

**#449
OPPOSING CAMPS
by Judith Arnold**

Read all the Calendar of Romance titles, coming to you one per month, all year, only in American Romance.

WELCOME TO

The quintessential small town where everyone knows everybody else!

Finally, books that capture the pleasure of tuning in to your favorite TV show!

GREAT READING...GREAT SAVINGS...AND A FABULOUS FREE GIFT!

Each book set in Tyler is a self-contained love story; together, the twelve novels stitch the fabric of the community. The covers honor the old American tradition of quilting; each cover depicts a patch of the large Tyler quilt.

With Tyler you can receive a fabulous gift ABSOLUTELY FREE by collecting proofs-of-purchase found in each Tyler book. And use our special Tyler coupons to save on your next TYLER book purchase.

Join your friends at Tyler for the sixth book, SUNSHINE by Pat Warren, available in August.

When Janice Eber becomes a widow, does her husband's friend David provide more than just friendship?

HARLEQUIN·

A M E R I C A N ◆ R O M A N C E ®

IF YOU THOUGHT
ROMANCE NOVELS WERE ALL
THE SAME . . . LOOK AGAIN!

Our exciting new look
begins this September

And now, Harlequin American Romance is better than ever!
Starting this September, Harlequin invites you to
experience the *new* American Romance. . . .
Bold, brash and exciting romantic adventures—where
anything is possible and dreams come true.

Also in September, look for our exciting new cover that will
whisk you into the world of fast-paced, romantic adventure.

Watch for a sneak preview of
our new covers next month!

HARLEQUIN AMERICAN ROMANCE—
Love was never so exciting!